S0-BJB-137

THE CHILDREN'S CORNER

THE CHILDREN'S CORNER

JACKSON TIPPETT MCCRAE

THE ENOLAM GROUP, INC.

This is a work of fiction. Any characters, places, events, and names used are fictitious. Any resemblance to actual events, locales, organizations, or persons, living or dead, is entirely coincidental and beyond the intent of either the author or publisher.

ISBN: 0-9715536-1-0

LCCN: 2004108694

First Printing

Printed in the United States on acid-free paper

Published by
The Enolam Group, Inc.

Book and cover design by The Enolam Group, Inc.

For Pam

CONTENTS

THE CHILDREN'S CORNER

Anne Marie hesitated before working her fat foot back into the bedroom shoe. It felt good to let her toes breathe; to free them from their terrycloth prison for these few moments. Picking at the flaking red nail polish prior to encasing her foot, she let her fingers linger over a large yellow corn. She knew she would have to do something about it eventually—she just didn't feel like tackling the job anytime soon. Besides, she was still at work and Clovis had yet to notice it each night when they crawled into bed together after a hard day at Bradshill's Furniture. She still had time to take care of the corn. Time before Clovis began to needle her about it.

She reached down to pull a black thread from the slipper, admiring at the same time the embroidered stitching on the top of her foot coverings. Then her gaze moved upward. She would have to shave her legs more closely. White, stubble-covered ankles stared up at her. Clovis didn't like it when her legs became embedded with the small stiff hairs. And her too-short stretch pants showed more than enough of her swollen lower calves. Tiny varicose veins had begun to form around the ankles—hundreds of purple-tinged tributaries leading nowhere. "Just like my life," she thought as she gazed around at the cheap furniture which filled the warehouse-like structure that took eight hours away from her each day.

The purple rivers were very much a part of the map of her and about the only thing that gave color to her skin. She was overweight, too white, and bloated with water retention and heft—the body of a forty-five-year-old woman. Too bad she didn't have something as outward and tangible as her varicose veins to point her in some direction. Some sign. Some hope. She knew where she had come from, but she didn't know where she was going, and the fact that she was in a loveless marriage with a violent and alcoholic husband didn't brighten her thoughts.

As she lifted herself up from the back-office sofa, the plastic covering stuck to her thighs (even through the pant material) so that she had to reach around with one globular arm and detach it. She would have to lose some weight. Clovis had complained about that also.

Anne Marie brushed the fallen bangs of her gentle brown hair back and let out a small stream of air from her pretty mouth. "Time to get back to work," she said under her breath as she made her way through the maze of cheap kitchen tables and recliners that vied for attention and space in the musty, badly-lit store. The furniture store was quiet at this time of day—the Saturday rush would come tomorrow. She sauntered over to the counter where the cash register, refrigerator, and boss—Mrs. Bradshill—were located. It was the only area of the store which was air-conditioned and even in October, the heat in Mississippi could be brutal. She welcomed this respite, and as she entered the area she noted how the cool air wafted over the layer of sweat that had formed on her skin.

"Look," Mrs. Bradshill was saying to Clovis in her pointed manner, stopping her counting of the cash register money momentarily to punctuate what she was about to say. She was leaning over the counter, her eyes intensely focused on Clovis, her arms folded in front of her, wrapping a soiled baby-blue sweater close to her chest. She reached up to straighten her glasses. "All I'm saying is that if someone hasn't paid me a cent for six whole months, then I'm fed up to the teeth. I'm not going to let anyone get away with that, I don't care how poor they are."

Mrs. Bradshill was tall, elegant, and always appeared well dressed, even if some of her clothes were a good twenty years old. Except for the occasional stains and threadbare patches, she always looked well put together. She was the type of person one thought of when the word "thrift" was used—she fit the definition perfectly. It was somewhat ironic to her customers that a woman of such assumed class and demeanor (it was said she came from money) would run a furniture store, let alone one which specialized in cheap recliners, badly made sofas, and tacky reproductions of lesser known oil paintings, their subjects almost always a spray of flowers or some poorly painted landscape. As she spoke to Clovis, the sound of Anne Marie's slippers slapping on the floor grew louder.

"Listen here. That old woman is 'bout the dirtiest, poorest woman I's ever seen and I'm *telling* you, I'm ain't a-going out *there* and pick that stuff up we delivered, I don't care what you says," shot Clovis in her direction. Every now and then he would accent words with a pointed finger, sticking his head forward and stamping one booted foot at the same time. "And if you want it back so bad you can get *him* to go out there and get it," and with that he jerked his thumb over in my direction and cut his eyes to me. "Besides," he went on, "last time I went out there I was sick in bed for a week. That place is filthy. Trust me. You ain't gonna want any of that furniture back, I don't care how much she owes you."

I had to agree with him on that point. The three of us, Clovis, Anne Marie, and me, had worked for Mrs. Bradshill now for over a year, with Clovis and Yours Truly delivering furniture to the inhabitants of rural Mississippi, and Anne Marie helping Mrs. Bradshill in the store with the less strenuous chores. None of us had ever experienced or heard of anything like it.

While Clovis and I had been the only ones to actually *see* the old woman and her trailer, Clovis had made sure he told Anne Marie and Mrs. Bradshill all about it as soon as we returned. Of course he had told Anne Marie more of the details later since Mrs. Bradshill wasn't one to want anything other than the big picture. That, plus the fact that for all of their fighting, Anne Marie and her husband were still somewhat close, as if they had some hidden bond the rest of us couldn't see.

While Anne Marie and Clovis were married officially, I was nevertheless constantly trying to decide if they were the most mismatched couple or the most perfectly matched one. They had some deep-seated underlying thread in common, but I couldn't put my finger on what it was. And yet, they say opposites attract, and maybe this was the reason for their involvement with each other. What did I know? I was only sixteen years old at the time. I wasn't aware yet of all the possibilities that the world held, but I *was* aware of how people lived—that much I had seen from visits to the customers of the store—and as many of these people weren't exactly well off, I used this information to gauge my family's standard of living, discovering in the process that we were upper middle class by comparison. I also discovered that, despite the fact Anne Marie and Clovis both worked for a living, they still weren't what you would call "well off." Mrs. Bradshill, it seems, didn't pay well, and while I was employed at the store as part of a high school work-study program (it enabled me to skip physical education classes taught by a rather sadistic coach Stoats) Clovis and Anne Marie *needed* the money.

Clovis was poor. Dirt poor, as his family had been migrant workers in Arkansas at one time. But Anne Marie, well, it was said that she came from money at one time—like Mrs. Bradshill. I tried to see it, searching her face, her clothes, anything for a sign of previous wealth, but I couldn't make out the remnants. It's like when you hear someone has cancer and you meet them again after being given that bit of information. You scrutinize the face, the body, the demeanor in an attempt to see what the disease has done so far to the individual, the whole time with the pretext of just being glad to see them. It was that way with Anne Marie. One was always looking for a ring, some piece of clothing from long ago that her parents might have bought her, some semblance of breeding. With Clovis everything was evident—right on top—no guessing there. But Anne Marie was an enigma, and while I found myself being attracted to anyone who had even remotely been connected to money, sophistication, or class in our small town, for some reason it was Clovis with whom I momentarily bonded. This was probably due to the fact that we shared more than one unusual experience in delivering furniture, the least of which wasn't the aforementioned trip to the woman's trailer—the very one Mrs. Bradshill wanted us to go to again.

I felt sorry for Clovis most of the time. He couldn't read or write, but Mrs. Bradshill had hired him because he was in need of a job. She didn't pay much to anyone, but she did have a big heart and gave Clovis a chance. It wasn't a matter of "Could he do the job," although he could. It was a matter of "He needed a job." You won't find that way of thinking much these days. For all of Mrs. Bradshill's thriftiness and hard exterior, she had a soft spot for some people—usually the underdog. The interesting thing about her was that you were always trying to figure out why she picked certain ones to help and then neglected others. It didn't seem to have anything to do with race or class or even the number of teeth an individual possessed—and in Mississippi this could be a major determining factor in relationships and class structure. This reason for her helping others seemed to transcend all logic. It was as if she had some sort of inner ability to judge people deep down and either reward them or reprimand them based on some psychic intellect. It seemed as if she knew certain people's *real* stories, and was just watching—waiting for them to fall into their own trap. She might have been running a furniture store on the surface, but in reality, it was strictly a theatre operation.

But that wasn't the way she was with Clovis. She had demonstrated by her actions that some part of her felt connected to him, or at least wanted to help. Clovis could be mean and rude, but she saw something in him, something different, and once she did, there was no turning back.

Clovis was about six feet tall with greasy silver hair which was close cropped on the sides and back, but full and hanging down in front, so that he looked like some fancy lapdog that had bitten his handler halfway through the grooming session and had been abandoned. His face was horse-like and his skin was weathered and marked by white blotches where the pigment seemed to retreat to some inner place. Parts of his neck looked like a map of Siberia. Each day he wore the same thing: blue-black workmen's pants, construction boots, and a short-sleeved shirt with a penguin over the left pocket. Winter and summer he wore a dark blue quilted jacket that sported numerous tears and patches. He always smelled of sour milk and he chain-smoked about three packs of unfiltered Pall Malls a day. It wasn't that I didn't like Clovis, but rather that he didn't like me. At least most of the time. I was just happy to have a job at sixteen and be free of the excessive pushups coach Stoats thought I should perform, simply because I played the piano and didn't spend time swearing or grabbing my crotch unnecessarily like most of the other boys my age. And because Clovis was a good thirty years older than me, I wanted to get along with him—respect for your elders—that sort of thing. I was all too aware of his shortcomings and the fact that I had been given a good education and that he hadn't, but I never made a point of bringing this up, regardless of how much he teased me and fought with me. He also tended to take charge of situations, like the one with the lady in the trailer, so I stepped out of his way and let him feel important. Besides, I didn't want to deal with what was inside that place. It was the one thing we agreed on.

Six months ago, Clovis and I had delivered a kitchen table, mattress, and box springs to the non-paying woman who lived several miles outside of town. She was inhabiting one of those silver, stainless steel-looking, one-room trailer homes from the thirties with no electricity or running water, even though this was 1975. The trip was indelibly etched on both our brains, as it had been even more out of the ordinary than some. Once, while making our delivery rounds, we had been met at the door by a frustrated housewife wearing only a feather boa and high heels. While Clovis had partaken of the offerings, I had remained in the cab of the truck, content to peruse the driver's manual for the 1965 Ford that was the company's mode of transporting furniture. But the day we delivered furniture to Mrs. Scruggs—the woman in the trailer—topped even that.

As we approached the door to the small home, we noticed a strange smell—nothing too strong, but just out of the ordinary, like a faint mixture of a veterinarian office and slaughterhouse on a hot summer day. Clovis had looked over at me, and all he said was, "Lordy, Lordy," while shaking his head the way I'd seen businessmen do who couldn't understand why their wife would want to go to a ballet or symphony orchestra concert in nearby Jackson.

"What's *that?*" I asked as he reached the top of three rickety metal steps leading up to the trailer's door. The top step was rusted almost completely into fragments, and the heel of Clovis's left boot sagged a good three inches precariously below where it should have rested. I looked around, waiting for him to answer. A thicket of pine trees surrounded the trailer and a gentle breeze came over them, scattering the past year's brown needles into the humid October afternoon. For a moment the smell went with it. Then it returned. It was desolately quiet in rural

Mississippi. There didn't seem to be any birds singing and it was as though all the wildlife in the area had moved away. Brown grass covered everything and the only vibrancy consisted of a few bright, primary-colored tubs and bins that farmers sometimes used as feeding troughs for the now non-existent farm animals.

"You just stand there and be quiet," was all he said. He balanced himself on the steps like a drunk, so I retreated and watched from near the truck. At that age I was still doing what I was told and it would be some time before I would talk back to someone of his position, regardless of the fact that he was illiterate. After a moment Clovis let loose, his weathered hand knocking on the door. In a booming voice full of authority and bravado he projected like a tenor at the Metropolitan Opera: "Delivery. Delivery for Mrs. . . ." He paused to look at the delivery sheet, but no sooner had he done so than it began. The moment Clovis's fist hit the door and his voice sang out, the life which had been hiding in the area made itself known.

Body language tells a great deal, and Clovis's actions spoke volumes. He jumped straight up in the air with good reason: The moment he announced himself, a multitude of dogs inside the trailer began to bark and yap wildly. He regained his composure, and as he now stood on the grass, below the step he had initially occupied while waiting for the door to open, he looked around to make sure I wasn't laughing. Then he approached the trailer again and stood on the bottom rung of the steps.

When the old woman finally came to the door, creaking open the rusted entryway with her arthritic hand, I saw Clovis move even faster than the few seconds before when the dogs let loose. As soon as the entrance had been opened a good three inches he let out a "Damn!" and flew back in my direction, his heel catching a chunk of metal step and snapping it off in crisp, potato-chip fashion. I was about to ask what the problem was as he came at me wild-eyed, but by the time he made it over to me, I realized what had sent him hurtling in my direction.

We both immediately brought our arms and sleeves to our noses as the sound of a multitude of dogs and cats filled the air, along with a powerful stench. Several of the animals spilled out into the yard, yapping and snarling before the woman could shut the door. Her meager attempt to relegate them to the inside of the trailer with her aging legs was an exercise in futility. After a moment she managed to close the door and descend the steps, barely noticing that several of her inmates had escaped into the withering underbrush. She was now standing in the front yard. The din within the small silver box maintained its volume and her stubby legs disappeared into the tall grass as the hem of her dirty housedress caught on a dead thistle growing up from the cinder-block foundation of the squalid domicile.

"You can just put my delivery anywhere in there over to the left side of the trailer," she said as she attempted to disentangle herself from the dried thistle. "Just be careful not to let any more of the animals out. I'll get some chicken wire from around back to hold them in while you do whatever it is you have to do," and with that she limped around the left side of the trailer, returning shortly with a large, gangly piece of rusted wire, the octagon designs mashed completely flat in some places and a plethora of dirty chicken feathers covering more than a third of its hoary surface. Something about her wasn't right—I mean, more than the obvious. Her speech. It wasn't Southern or rural enough, especially for someone living as she was.

Clovis shot me a look and we headed to the back of the truck to unhinge the gate. "Just take a deep breath before you go in," he said. "We're going to throw this stuff in there and then get the hell outa here."

Somehow the old woman had reentered her home with only two cats escaping, and we could hear her machinations as she herded the animals over to one side of the trailer. It rocked slightly from the commotion inside, like a school bus full of impatient kids on their way to an outing at a museum or amusement park. The last two cats that had escaped gently picked their way through a rather rusted and dangerous series of blades which had previously belonged to some form of farm machinery. It stuck out from under the trailer—a giant, decaying monster on which the temporary housing had landed; a huge claw turned upwards toward the late afternoon sky.

I grabbed one end of the kitchen table and we started for the trailer. As we neared the door, Clovis held the table by one hand and attempted to turn the cheap, rattling doorknob with the other. My timing was thrown off as I waited for Clovis to get inside with his end of the furniture, and I sucked in a deep breath too late. Since I was close to the door my lungs filled with the putrid smell and I had to hold it in while we set the table down among newspapers, cat excrement, and yelping dogs.

As soon as the table legs hit the floor I bolted for the outside. Managing to reach the far end of the trailer I hurled the entire contents of my stomach into a patch of dead milkweed. While I was bent over in agony, my mind had time to replay the scene I had witnessed inside the trailer. Continuing to retch, I recalled the sound of what seemed to be a hundred dogs, their feet tearing about the newspaper-covered floor. Their yelping seemed to be as real as any cry of a human for help.

For some reason, two images had burned themselves into my brain the few moments I was in the trailer: dried cat excrement overhanging the side of a pot on the stove, and a large blue Persian sitting high on one of the bookshelves, placidly staring down at us with a disdain usually reserved for Frenchmen looking at tourists. About this time Clovis came around the side of the trailer.

"I'll be okay in a minute," I said. I felt his hand on my shoulder for a second as if to say that he understood, and then he walked back to the truck to pull the mattress off. I thought how odd it was that he had touched me. He had never done that before. Clovis, whom I thought was immune to emotion and feelings. He didn't approve or want to stick around, but he somehow understood.

After a few minutes I joined him. Neither of us said a word, but my timing was better this go-around as we lifted the mattress, and I managed to fill my lungs with semi-clean air. Before I knew it we were done and heading back to the store. It's amazing what adversity will do. Clovis and I had shared some bizarre experiences delivering furniture, but this one was the worst.

"I'm never going back to that shit hole," he said while lighting up one of his cigarettes. "Boy, you sure made a mess back there," and he took his eyes off the road for a second to look at me.

I didn't say anything. I just sat there feeling humiliated. I didn't even feel sorry for the woman. It was one thing to be poor. It was one thing to care for animals. But it was just plain ignorance to live in the conditions she was tolerating. Besides, most of the animals looked half starved to death. She wasn't really caring for them in my opinion.

"Maybe we should call the ASPCA?" I said, trying to rejoin the living.

"Hell, they don't care around here. Besides, what are they going to do? I'll tell you what. They'll just take them animals outa there and in a week or so they'll all be dead. Gassed," and he made a slicing motion across his throat with his right hand while his left steadied the steering wheel of the truck.

So that was the reason neither of us wanted to return to repossess the furniture. Forget the fact that the old woman had never paid a cent on her deliveries. Who would want them back anyway? They were probably covered with urine and feces from every animal within a hundred miles.

"Look," Mrs. Bradshill was saying, still trying to convince Clovis to go back, "the sheriff says that he can't do anything until I at least try to reclaim the goods. And I can't call the old woman because she doesn't have a phone."

"Phone, hell, she doesn't have any electricity," interjected Clovis. About this time Anne Marie made an appearance at his side and slid one of her flabby arms around his waist. He firmly gripped it and moved it away. She just looked hurt and waddled off to the back storeroom.

"If you ask me, I think you just want to make my life miserable," continued Clovis in response to Mrs. Bradshill's last remark as he wrestled a recliner back into formation. It now rejoined the other fourteen chairs which were in a straight row, lining the walkway from the front of the store to the back. "You know as well as I do that all that stuff is ruined. There ain't nothing you can do with it now. Hell, I'll pay you for it myself rather than go out there and suffer through that again."

"It's the principle of the thing, Clovis," said Mrs. Bradshill, and stared him down. There was a moment of uneasy silence between the two.

"All I know is that I've got some more deliveries to make today and I'll think about it, but I wouldn't hold my breath if I were you, and no pun intended," and with that he strode off to the front of the store, motioning for me over his shoulder. I just gave Mrs. Bradshill a look that said, "I can't do a thing with him."

When I caught up with Clovis he was struggling to free an orange burlap-covered colonial sofa from a row of even less attractive ones.

"She's just lost her mind, completely," he said to the middle cushion. And then stacking all three together, he continued addressing them: "Who does she think she is? She can't order us to go out there. It's inhumane. That's what it is. Everybody in town says that old woman in the trailer is crazy. Hell, she's only lived there for the past nine months. Nobody knows where she come from and all. I'd just as soon not fool with her *or* the damn furniture."

As usual, I kept quite. Clovis almost never wanted a conversation. He wanted to talk, but he didn't want a conversation. If I ever did venture to say something, he usually made fun of it. It struck me as odd that someone who was older and had virtually no education would make fun of an adolescent boy who, for all practical purposes, had been relatively well educated but didn't feel the need to flaunt it. I was on the way to finishing high school and Clovis had dropped out of the third grade to work and support what was left of his family. I would eventually come to realize exactly what had been going on in Clovis's mind. Well, at least most of it. At that moment though, I was still confused.

I learned early on in our relationship not to cross Clovis. Once, during the first week of my employment at Bradshill's Furniture, I had been writing something down—a note, a reminder, I can't remember—and it had contained the word "knife" in it. I hadn't thought much of the note until I saw Clovis standing over it, trying to read it. Knowing that he could make out a few letters and sounds I figured that he was just trying to better himself, practicing every chance he could get. Either that or he was so paranoid that he thought I had written something about him. Optimism dies a slow death at sixteen.

He squinted at the paper for the longest time. When I came around to the back of the counter where the cash register was, he thrust the paper out at me, and with one of his dry, cracked fingers, pointed to one of the words I had written.

"What's this word, here?" he asked and looked at me intensely. I could tell he was in a bad mood, so I didn't pretend it was something it wasn't. Ordinarily I might have told him, "Oh, that's Madagascar, or venereal disease," but today I simply told him the truth. I've found this small, but useful ploy—to tell the truth—has the most profound effect on people from time to time. Once when I was fourteen, my mother knocked on my firmly locked bedroom door. She asked me what I was doing, and so I told her. She never asked again.

Remembering the impact of that incident, I looked up at Clovis and answered him: "Knife," I said, and proceeded to make change for myself out of the cash register. Only Mrs. B and I were allowed to make change or prepare the bank bag at the end of the day. I'm sure this had at least something to do with Clovis's animosity toward me, him being so much older and presumably more responsible, at least in his mind. Mrs. Bradshill and Anne Marie were at the front of the store, and since the cash register was at the back and Clovis felt safely out of view, he decided to use this opportunity to taunt me.

"Nuh-uh," he said and his eyes glowed red. "Ain't no word like knife spelled with a *K*. I knows what a *K* looks like. You think I'm stupid? I know knife is spelled with an *N*. Ain't no *K* in the word."

I was not immune to his insults and they occasionally got the better of me. Sometimes when I wasn't guarding every moment, my mind ran on automatic and my mouth said what my brain was thinking.

This could be dangerous in the South.

This would be one of those moments.

"Knife is spelled with a *K*," I said, nonchalantly counting out ten brand-new ones onto the counter. I rested my left hand on the oiled, unpainted plywood surface next to the register after I had finished, lost in thought. As I looked up toward the front of the store I replied, "I don't really care whether you believe me or not." It wasn't that I was being antagonistic toward Clovis, but rather that I was momentarily in another world, thinking about school and a recent piano lesson I had suffered through last week—one in which my teacher and I had argued over which school I would attend when I graduated. I had thought about studying privately with a teacher in St. Louis. She thought otherwise. I had studied piano since I was five, my goal being to play professionally someday. I imagined thrilling crowds at Carnegie Hall with my latest rendition of Rachmaninoff's Second Piano Concerto or the more familiar Tchaikovsky.

In what I consider to be the luckiest timing of my life, I decided to remove my left hand from the counter at just the right moment. One second longer and I would have seen it crucified like a butterfly onto the plywood, for Clovis had, in record time, located an enormous Phillips screwdriver and brought it down with such force over my left hand, that it was now sticking completely through the two-inch-thick plywood top.

I stared at him in horror as his eyes glowed and he whispered the words, "Spelled with an *N*. Ain't no *K*," the *N*, and *K*, being especially loudly expelled.

Completely shaken by this most recent act of violence, I slowly walked out from behind the cash register and found one of the cheap velveteen swivel chairs to sit in. I had only been there a minute when Mrs. Bradshill walked by and wanted to know why I was sitting down on the job. I opened my mouth but no words came out, so I got up and went into the back storeroom to see if I could help Anne Marie with anything. I was still in shock over the fact that I had almost lost the use of one of my hands.

So that was Clovis. You didn't cross him. He was unpredictable. He was insecure. He drank too much and he probably beat his wife. Not that I didn't have my own problems, but at least I never took a Phillips screwdriver to anyone's hand.

While Clovis could be downright violent, Anne Marie was the other extreme. At first I thought she was just an overly nice person, but I slowly began to realize that her affection wasn't directed at everyone—it was mainly reserved for me. While talking to me about her Pekinese or tiger lily bulbs, she would reach out and grasp my forearm for about two point five seconds too long. She seemed to linger, and occasionally I would have to feign some excuse for moving away from her. So it wasn't without trepidation that I went into the storeroom on this day to help her, just as I had done the day of Clovis's tirade. It seemed to me to be the lesser of two evils at the time. It was either that or risk having a screwdriver punched through some other part of my body whenever I disagreed with her husband.

I found her dusting several rolls of plastic-wrapped carpeting. Anne Marie wasn't the brightest bulb in the light fixture of life, but she was, at the moment, an improvement over Clovis. "Mrs. Bradshill said I should come back here and see if I could help you," I lied.

I found some packing material in a corner and began to separate it in order to make long strips so that I could wrap the legs of some of the end tables. They were constantly getting banged up with Clovis's rough handling and the customers had been complaining.

"So have you been practicing much lately?" asked Anne Marie seductively as her feather duster lazily grazed the tops of the carpet rolls.

"Nah," I said. "I've had a lot of homework to do and this job takes up most of my time after school. I'm going to really get busy on it this summer when I have more time."

Anne Marie wasn't that bad, I guess. You just had to know how to handle her—how to take her a bit at a time. She really did have a motherly quality underneath her outwardly sugary and sometimes obsequious exterior.

"Mrs. Bradshill says you're pretty good—that you could really do something with your talent some day. Says you won a competition over in Meridian last year." She moved sideways like a soft stuffed crab, her bedroom shoes kicking up clouds of dust as she painted the feather plume over cylindrical shapes of faded linoleum lining the wall.

I thought about how Clovis had tried to insert a twelve-inch screwdriver through my hand and what effect this would have had on my piano-playing abilities and I winced. "I don't know," I said, "one person tells you you're pretty good and the next one is unimpressed. I don't know what to believe." I tried to concentrate on my work, tying several ominous-looking rubber bands around the soft cushiony material I had wrapped around one of the maple end table legs.

"You know, my sister is a concert pianist," said Anne Marie somewhat out of the blue. I just sat there watching her duster move up and down like a soft painter's brush. "Yeah," she went on, never taking her eyes from her task, "she lives in Chicago. I know what you're thinking. What happened to me, right? You'd never know that I come from a well-to-do family. My sister really made something of herself, but I'm afraid that I've been one big disappointment to my family. They disowned me when I married Clovis."

"That was mean," I said, trying to sound sympathetic and at the same time guarded. I wasn't totally sure if she was telling the truth. It seemed somewhat fantastic, but then, so had most things in my life up to that point.

"I could have had anyone. Been anything. Lord knows I was given enough chances. But then I met Clovis and fell in love."

I asked her what her sister's name was to see if I had ever heard of her. Not that that meant anything. The world is full of great pianists that no one has heard of. Besides, even if she wasn't as great as Anne Marie said, she was living in Chicago and probably had access to mounds of culture that I could only imagine. I eyed Anne Marie from the back, trying to imagine her in a wealthy household with a less ample frame and better manners. Maybe she had slid downhill at an early age? Maybe marrying Clovis had changed her? How long ago had it happened anyway? And to end up here, in Flora, Mississippi, of all places. Was love really that strong? And Clovis wasn't exactly a prize. The whole thing seemed bizarre to me, but then, I really didn't have much else to go on at the time.

"I'll give you my sister's address and you can write to her," she said as she moved in the direction of a pile of sofas wrapped in heavy brown paper. She began to gingerly dust the umber mounds, careful to sweep any debris onto the floor in front of the sofas so that she could later collect it with one of the pastel-colored plastic dustpans hanging by the door.

"This is bizarre," I thought to myself. "She could be lying. But why would she take a chance such as this and give me her sister's address if she were making the story up? Surely she realizes that I would find out the truth?"

"That would be great," I said, responding to her offer of the address and I began putting the finishing touches on the base of a floor lamp. I stood back to admire my work. The mummified pole was now a good three inches thicker than when I had begun. It probably wasn't necessary, but it kept me away from Clovis and his screwdriver collection.

I didn't give Anne Marie's sister much thought for the rest of that day—Clovis and I had several deliveries to make and not much time to make them in—so I was somewhat surprised when Anne Marie handed me an envelope with her sister's address on it, just before closing. She pressed it into my hand as we were all leaving the store, as though we were two third-graders writing each other, afraid of being caught by the teacher.

Mrs. Bradshill's right arm was wrapped tightly around the bank bag containing that day's receipts as she herded us toward the front of the store. "Clovis, make sure you turn off the lights in back of the store," she called to the rear of the building as she observed Anne Marie give me the envelope. I looked up at her. "Anne Marie's sister's address," I said, thinking I needed to explain why Anne Marie and I were exchanging bits of paper somewhat clandestinely. "Hmmm," was all she said.

Of course, one of the first things I did was to sit down and write Anne Marie's sister a letter. It went something like this:

Dear Miss Plazinoff:

You don't know me, but I know your sister Anne Marie. We work together in a furniture store in Flora, Mississippi. I hope you don't mind me writing to you as Anne Marie said you wouldn't.

I am a pianist living here in Mississippi who would one day like to make my living at performing. Since you already do this, I was wondering if you could give me some advice on how to proceed with a career.

Currently I am working on several pieces with my piano teacher, Mrs. Hanson. I plan to play a recital next summer in which I will be performing Debussy's "Children's Corner." I'm sure you are familiar with the piece.

I would love to hear from you and would be grateful for any advice you can give me. Thank you.

I signed my name, checked the address again, and put more than the needed postage on the envelope—I didn't want to take any chances that the letter wouldn't reach the intended person. Anne Marie had told me that her sister wasn't married; that Plazinoff was their family name and the one she had before marrying Clovis. Finding the name rather unusual, I made sure I spelled it correctly. After all, it wasn't a name you ran into around these parts, but then, Anne Marie was from Chicago.

A week went by with no response. Clovis and I made several deliveries a day and he constantly fought with Mrs. Bradshill about everything, the least of which wasn't the repossession of the old lady's furniture. Clovis was adamant that he wasn't going back to the trailer and be subjected to the filth of the place. I couldn't have agreed more. He continued his usual teasing of me and I continued my usual silence.

Then one day before work, I made my way to the mailbox at home and extracted the monthly bills, the usual junk mail, and various other odds and ends. While I was going through this mélange of correspondence I noticed a familiar-looking letter. It took a second for the facts to register—that it was my handwriting I was viewing. Then it became clear: My letter had boomeranged back to me with "Return to Sender—No such address," marked on it in broken and faded red ink. A printed hand, like the ones in old-time advertisements, pointed to the offending script. Immediately I checked the address Anne Marie had given me. It matched. "What could be wrong?" I thought. Maybe she had made a mistake in writing it down? Maybe they really didn't speak that much and she couldn't remember her sister's address verbatim, off the top of her head? I didn't think she had made her sister up. After all, didn't she know I would write, and if her sister didn't exist, wouldn't I find out?

The next day at the store I casually mentioned to Anne Marie that the letter had come back. "I must have written down the wrong address or something," I said, trying to give her the benefit of the doubt as we stood there among the plastic-covered Sealy Posturepedics.

"Let me see," she said, taking the envelope from my hand. I had brought it to the store to show her the postal markings that refused delivery. "Ohhhh," she cooed while putting one of her fingernails to her lips. "It's forty-four eighty-four, not forty-eight eighty-four for the street address. I must have written it down wrong. I'm sorry," and she handed me back the envelope with more than the necessary smile.

Well, that explained it. A simple mistake. I would just take the letter I had already written out of the first envelope and put it into another one with the correct address. I did this and sent it the next day, again, forgetting all about it with the week's deliveries.

That week we made the usual kind of runs: a kitchen table to the Hamiltons; a recliner to Old Man Richardson; a mattress and box springs to a newlywed couple who had been so happy in their marital bliss that they hadn't noticed they didn't even have a bed yet. It always interested me to see inside other people's houses. Well, most of them. Mrs. Bradshill was still hounding Clovis to go and repossess the old lady's furniture, but he was standing firm. "I wouldn't go out there for a hunert dollars," he finally said and stomped out of the store to smoke a cigarette. I went outside to speak with him. It wasn't something I would have normally done, but I didn't know where else to turn.

The last letter to Anne Marie's sister had been returned, again with the same, "Return to sender—No such address," and I was becoming suspicious. I eased over to Clovis, who eyed me with some distrust.

"I'm glad we don't have to go out there," I said, staring out at the highway traffic as it whizzed by the parking lot.

"At least we agree on one thing," he said as he leaned up against a supporting column of the store's façade. One ankle was crossed over the other and his hand containing the cigarette hung loosely at his side. He stared straight ahead, only occasionally cutting his glance over to me to make sure I hadn't moved or grown an extra limb or shaved my head or something.

I decided to try and approach the subject of Anne Marie's sister in some indirect way.

"Clovis," I began, "I know we haven't always gotten along and sometimes you think I'm a real do-nothing, but I need some advice." I really didn't know what other approach to take with him, and I've always found that you can be sworn enemies with a person, but the minute you ask their advice, they become so ego filled and blown up that they forget all about previous differences and start full throttle into whatever it was you wanted to know.

"Okay," he said, eyeing me suspiciously.

"It's about girls," I said, lying.

"You need to be askin' somebody else about that and not me," he said, and took an exceptionally long drag on his cigarette while his eyes seemed to focus on a gray metal transformer located in the middle of the parking lot. He eyed it with unusual interest. I had made him nervous.

"I'm asking because I think you've probably had a lot of experience," I lied again.

He kicked the sidewalk shyly and then stubbed out his cigarette which he had thrown down with more than the needed dose of masculine bravado.

"Well, I have had some . . . here and there," he said, straightening himself up for the first time that day and smiling impishly.

"Well," I went on, "what I want to know is, how long did you know Anne Marie before you got married? I mean, what is the length of time a person should know someone before they marry them? I mean, do they have to know the person's family and all?" I knew I had him. I didn't give a hoot about the length of time you needed to know someone, I just wanted to know how long he had known Anne Marie and if he had ever met her sister.

"Let's see, Anne Marie and I knew each other . . . well, it was only about six or seven months before we got married."

"Did you have to meet her family before they allowed you to get married?"

"Now, look here," he said turning to me, thinking that he had figured out where the conversation was headed, "you're entirely too young to get married and if you're even thinkin' about it, I'd just as soon run in there and tell Mrs. Bradshill so as she can tell your folks. Don't be messin' around with gettin' any girl pregnant at your age—not that you even could," and he eyed me up and down as he lit up another cigarette.

I didn't want to lose him, so I swallowed my pride, or rather what little there was of it at that age. "I'm just asking for future reference. Sorry," I said, "I didn't mean to get you all upset. It's just that most of my friends aren't very mature and you seem to have a lot of knowledge in the area," I continued, trying not to gag on my words.

He straightened up again. "Well, if you want to know the truth, I ain't never met Anne Marie's parents. They thought she was too good for me. They wouldn't come to the wedding or nuthin'. I don't know who they thought they were—being so uppity and all." He glanced around the parking lot with squinted eyes, obviously smarting from the pain these memories caused him. I pressed on.

"What about her sister? Didn't she want you guys to get married?"

"Never met her sister either," he went on, "though she's supposed to be some high-and-mighty piano player. You might ask Anne Marie for her address, though I doubt she'd write you back. I tried to get Anne Marie to let me get in touch with her parents and sister before we was married but she wasn't for it. Said they didn't want anything to do with her *or* me."

"They must have been pretty rich, huh?" I went on, hoping to get more information.

"Stinking rich. Chicago snobs if you ask me. Living in a thirty-room mansion with servants, swimming pools, tennis courts, the works. Why Anne Marie would want to leave all that and come live with me I'll never know, but she did."

"Did you ever get to see where they lived? I mean, drive by and honk the horn or anything?"

"No. Anne Marie just told me about them. We met in Peru, not Chicago."

"Peru! What were you doing in Peru?" I asked incredulously, thinking that perhaps I had misjudged Clovis for the short time I had known him. I had imagined him as a country bumpkin with no education and no knowledge of the world, and now I was finding out that the man had traveled to South America. What other valuable nuggets lay in store for me under that seemingly rustic exterior?

He looked at me as if I had two heads, sticking his neck out at me. "Why wouldn't I be in Peru?" he asked, somewhat hurt as he wobbled his neck back into place. He looked like an aged turtle in the afternoon light.

"Nothing," I said, "It's just that . . . well, South America is so far away and don't you have to speak Spanish or something?"

"What the hell are you talking about?" He turned in my direction and was facing me now, clearly over his momentary arthritic and reptilian moment. "I swear you can be the dumbest thing this side of the Rio Grande. Peru ain't in no South America. It's in Illinois! Anybody knows that."

"Peru, Illinois?" I asked.

"Right next to La Salle." He took a drag on a new cigarette he had lit. "Don't they teach you geography in school nowadays?" he asked in a sarcastic tone. "Your questions is getting on my nerves," he said, and at that point he turned and walked back into the store, flinging his cigarette to the ground in disgust.

I was adding it all up. Clovis had never met Anne Marie's parents or her sister. I still had the returned envelope in my pocket but I didn't want to confront Anne Marie just yet. What if I was wrong? What if there really was a sister and I was just a screw-up when it came to mailing things? I've always tried to give people room for doubt, but in this case I was getting suspicious. I stood outside watching the highway cars fly by, and after a few moments decided I'd better get back to work.

I walked back into the store and made my way to where Clovis and Mrs. Bradshill were now standing. Clovis was a strange person—he was like the wind. He blew this way one minute and that way the next. You could never tell what he was going to do or why he was going to do it. His motivations were as distant and far-fetched as anything, so when he announced that we were going to repossess the old woman's furniture, you could have knocked me over with Anne Marie's feather duster.

"That was quick," I said. "How much money did she have to give you?" I went on, trying to get even for his latest comments about my intelligence and reproductive capabilities.

"You just shut up. Mrs. Bradshill ain't give me no money."

"Well, she must have done some very powerful and quick persuading," I said. "You were only in there with her for a few minutes."

Clovis only glared at me as his heavy boots beat down on the hard tiled floor of the store. "Anne Marie!" he bellowed, "we're going to Old Lady Scruggs. You said you wanted to go and see for yourself how that old lady lived. Well, you better get yourself together. We're leaving in two minutes whether you're there or not," and with that he swung out the front door and began to pile blankets into the back of the truck for the purpose of protecting what might be left of the repossessed furniture when it was removed.

After a moment or two, Anne Marie came waddling out of the store. While she waited for Clovis to get the truck ready, she took out a small baby-blue compact, flipped it open, and began to watch herself as she applied a thick coating of cherry-red lipstick to her small mouth. When she was done she returned the cosmetics to her purse and made her way into the front seat of the truck.

The three of us huddled in the front of the cab with Anne Marie in between Clovis and myself. I couldn't help but feel that Anne Marie had decided to inch her ample frame closer to me on purpose, if not for anything else, the fact that it would make me more uncomfortable. I still hadn't said anything about the letter. Why Anne Marie would want to go out with us and see this old woman's trailer was beyond me, but she did. It had probably been Clovis's constant references to the circus-like atmosphere of the place that intrigued her. He had tried to explain to her about the stench, but she wouldn't listen. Now, as I thought about the letter, a part of me felt she might get what she deserved. After all, maybe Clovis would let her go up and open the door.

The truck bumped along the back roads seemingly seeking out every pothole and washed-out rut. None of us spoke and I felt a palpable uneasiness come over me because of the fact that Anne Marie had insisted she accompany us. It was as if she wanted to see a freak show, and although I felt the experience of a poverty-stricken woman with several hundred cats and dogs in a one-room trailer was sad, I didn't think it merited carnival rubbernecking by parties unrelated. And I was considering forgiving her for the letter incident, thinking that I might have misjudged her. Optimism again.

"When we get there, you stay in the cab," said Clovis to Anne Marie, although it seemed as if he were addressing a car trying to pass on his left. He looked out at it and scowled, then honked the horn and cursed in their direction even though the motorist hadn't done anything wrong. Anne Marie didn't respond and I just looked out at the passing fields of dead brown grass and silhouetted trees. Occasionally a horse's tail swished in the distance, giving a bit of life to the winding-down day.

When we pulled up to the trailer, I knew something was wrong. Clovis and I opened our doors simultaneously as if we had rehearsed the motion for hours, and I let him move in front of me as we made our way up to the front door. The din coming from inside the trailer was enormous, reminding me of one of those early cartoons where the dogs are chasing cats around in circles, complete with canned music and stars and dust flying everywhere. Quite a change from our first approach when there had been nothing but silence.

I heard a noise behind me and out the corner of my eye I saw Anne Marie quietly sliding out of the cab of the truck. She attempted to ease the door shut with childlike girlish grace, closing the door with her wrists in order not to smear her newly painted fingernails, the whole time sticking her large rear end out. Clovis was oblivious to her and was by now banging on the door, adding to the commotion within. If any of the dogs hadn't been barking before, they were now with the assault of Clovis's fist on the thin metal door.

His fist rang out, slightly denting the cheap textured covering of the portal. Anne Marie crept up behind us as silently as she could, finding patches of soft grass to step on, purposely avoiding the dry, gravely areas of the yard. She held a fat bejeweled finger up to her pursed lips as if to say, "This is just our secret." I didn't say anything. I was still smarting from the incident with her make-believe sister, and while I vacillated between forgiveness and suspicion, I wanted to stay as emotionally clear from her as possible.

Clovis's fist rang out again and then he turned to me and said, "I'm going in. Hell, I don't care if she's home or not. If she ain't, then we'll just grab the things and be gone." Then he turned back toward the door and his hand gripped the rickety knob. It seemed that the moment I heard the square of metal wrench itself away from the frame of the trailer, everything went into slow motion.

The opening of an airplane door at thirty thousand feet would probably be only slightly less dramatic than that of the small trailer door on that fall day. Nothing could have prepared any of us for what lay in store, for no sooner had Clovis cracked the door an inch, than the paws of ten or twelve cats and dogs stuck themselves in the aperture he had created, trying desperately to free themselves from their prison.

Then came their muzzles and wild eyes as their hard heads strained to maximize the crack in the door. Dogs of every conceivable shape and size pressed their heads into the tiny opening. It seemed that their eyes would pop from their skulls as they strained at the opening, their skin pulled back tight because of the small space they were trying to squeeze through. Many appeared to be covered with something dull and brown and dried.

Before Clovis knew what was happening, the animals had forced the door open and were spilling into the yard like a bad comedy routine. And it would have been funny for at least a moment if it had not been for the smell. Clovis and I had thought the stench was bad before, but this time there was something different. This time there was something ominous.

As the animals cleared the trailer—all except a few cats which languished here and there on the top of cabinets and bookshelves or huddled underneath broken chairs, hissing their distrust—our senses adjusted to the air, the light, and the horror which lay before us.

Clovis was the first to see it, even though we were both looking in the same direction. It may have been that I was in denial that such a thing could take place, that I could be a witness to something so horrific. It was the same way I had felt when I had seen the returned envelope from Anne Marie's sister. I knew what I was seeing, but it took a moment for it to register. When it had done so, I was more than distraught.

Clovis turned to me in a moment of fear, his chest pushing me back out the door and down the steps. Gracefulness can't be calculated at moments like this, and as a result, both Clovis and I tumbled into the yard on top of each other, leaving the doorway unobstructed for Anne Marie who had seen the look on our faces, and, like any female, needed to know the reason.

She stepped quickly up to the door, seemingly impervious to the smell, and was already inside the claustrophobic trailer when we heard her scream. As she retreated she made it to the side of the truck before she fainted, and as Clovis had now regained his upright stature and ran toward her, he caught her and we both managed to lay her out on the grass.

"Lordy, Lordy, Lordy," was all Clovis could say. He was shaking and I had never seen him this upset, but to tell the truth,

I wasn't far behind. Then it began to dawn on us that what we had seen was real and not just some warped hallucination.

Evidently, because of the old woman's lack of perception in matters of feeding and caring for a large number of animals, she had grossly mistaken her role in that enclosed environment. Because they were so ill-fed and cared for, there was probably no love lost between them and her, and when she died of a heart attack a week earlier, the multitude of dogs and cats, having nothing to eat and deciding that no one was coming to their rescue, had gnawed large pieces out of the woman.

Indeed, when we first walked in, both Clovis and I had thought that there had been a gruesome murder. Her intestines were strewn a good three feet from her body and large sections of her heart and lungs were visible, the blood having been drained onto the surrounding newspapers.

Oddly enough, the old woman's face was almost completely intact from the animals mauling, but her wide eyes stared at us, covered by flies. Maggots crawled out from her mouth and nose and her white-yellowed hair seemed to have become a nest for some type of heaving insects.

Neither Clovis nor I had become sick at the sight and smell of her. Probably the shock was too great at the time. But when Anne Marie recovered from her fainting spell, she was up on her knees for almost thirty minutes, retching into the front yard while holding onto the rim of an abandoned tire. The now-defunct car part which supported her weight had been cut in the shape of tulip petals, surrounding a bed of dead iris. The limp rubbery leaves of the flowers acquiesced to Anne Marie's weighted arm as she unconsciously relaxed onto them, leaning over into the rim while her fleshy back heaved up and down, straining at the shiny peach material that covered her upper torso. A small bracelet on her wrist glistened in the sun.

When she was finally able to speak and only produce the occasional dry heaves, she looked up at Clovis. To this day I don't recall every having seen a more pitiful, tear-stained face that was more pathetic and helpless. Clovis too seemed taken aback, never before having seen her quite this upset.

But it hadn't been just the sight of a dead body partially eaten by a multitude of cats and dogs that had upset Anne Marie. It had been something much more, for when she reached out to Clovis and grasped his arm with the strength of a wrestler, looking into his eyes with a fear that I was never again to see in my life, she made clear to us that the other shoe had yet to drop.

"Clovis," she said tearfully to him as he knelt on one knee providing emotional and physical support, "Clovis . . . " and she choked back as much of the emotion as she could, completely forgetting previous tales she had woven for the multitudes over the years about her past, her relatives, her upbringing, as there was no time now for putting on airs, no time for pretending, no time for holding on to pretensions, "Clovis, take me back to the store," she managed to spill out with her eyes wide and round, and then she collapsed sobbing into his arms.

Clovis just stared at her. He looked up at me the same way Anne Marie had looked up at him, but there was nothing I could do. I just looked back.

Later, after the sheriff and coroner had inspected the scene and we had returned to the store (there was no more business conducted that day as Mrs. Bradshill seemed to think that all parties had better take the rest of the day off) we all seemed to be in a state of shock. While we could have gone home, no one did, as if held back by some natural disaster that has momentarily caused a group of people to bond. It was as if we needed to stay, to get the thing through. That and morbid curiosity held us fast.

Anne Marie sat in the back storeroom with a faded pink dog blanket—previous property of Mrs. Bradshill's poodle, Bidi—around her shoulders, drinking instant chicken soup from a large styrofoam cup. Clovis was at her side, his large rough hand resting on her shoulder, afraid that if he moved she would disappear. For a long while, she just sat there, hysterically silent, in shock, staring into space like someone pulled from the icy Atlantic after a shipwreck.

It was a few hours later that the story came spilling out from Anne Marie. We found out what the truth was when, as Mrs. Bradshill walked into the back storeroom to return one of her overly decorated lamps (mauve ceramic base with faux-gold ormolu mounts, hideous pastel-colored ceramic flowers) to its box, Anne Marie glanced up and simply began spewing her life's history in the direction of the lamp.

Mrs. Bradshill just stood there, not moving a muscle. I was standing at the cash register, counting out that day's receipts and money for the bank as the verbiage began to cascade out of her like torrents pitching over a waterfall. I could see her from the corner of my eye as I had a skewed, *Cabinet of Dr. Calagari* sort of view in the dim light of the storeroom.

"Five, ten, fifteen," I said to myself softly, not wanting them to know I was listening. And then her story:

"I knew she was looking for me, ever since I left home. We had always had such fights. I hated her and I loved her, being poor, not coming from money," Anne Marie was saying as she slowly rocked back and forth, her eyes now fixed on a bad painted cardboard rendition of Jesus and sheep located on the wall opposite her.

"Thirty-five, forty, forty-five," I continued, not wanting to break the spell.

"I never wanted you to know the truth about me," she said, looking up pleadingly at Clovis. "I wanted you to think I had come from somewhere, been somebody. I never meant to hurt you or anybody. And now she's dead. And to die such a horrible way, and living in that squalor. I had no idea she was here, no idea that she was living out there, probably spying on me when she got a chance," and at that moment she began to sob into Clovis's filth-covered jacket, her head turned sideways but her body still facing Jesus.

When she had regained herself somewhat after this latest spell, she resumed the story. "I ran away ten years ago. I thought it would be easier for everyone," she continued as a baby blue tissue appeared in front of her, seemingly from nowhere, but in reality attached to Mrs. Bradshill's right hand. "I thought she would be able to take care of herself (takes tissue). I never dreamed she would come looking for me. And to find her like that. All alone. Torn apart. My own mother." And then another more hysterical and silent pause before the rains began again.

"Oh, God, what have I done?" she threw out, fixated once again on the picture of Jesus. Her head was slightly thrown back and her wide eyes were framed with globs of running mascara.

Mrs. Bradshill didn't say anything, but slipped out of the room, probably hoping everyone would think she wanted to give Anne Marie and Clovis their privacy.

"Sixty, sixty-five, seventy," I went on, but more softly.

Clovis just kept his hand on her shoulder. Through the front windows of the store I could see an orange-and-red-streaked sky beginning to lower itself on the town. It was the usual sunset, full of faraway glory. It seemed to warm the whole room, and yet it had a lonely quality about it today. It always seemed that I was looking at it while it happened in some other land—never here.

"Eighty-five, ninety."

The rays from that day's dying sun streamed into the store among the cheap furniture, the dusty appliances, the yellowed rolls of linoleum lined up against the walls like bored old men with hands in their pockets on a Saturday night waiting for something to happen. It made its way up the center isle and found its place on the back wall, directly behind me. The hum of a distant refrigerator became more apparent. A lone piece of cardboard slid to the floor somewhere in the store with no hint of what had caused its movement.

"Ninety-five, a hundred," I said as softly as an "amen" in church.

I didn't look up.

It was closing time. Hopefully no more customers would be coming. We would all be going home soon, but as Mrs. Bradshill walked to the front of the store to lock the doors, just to make sure any late-coming patrons wouldn't try to gain entry, the soft moaning which Anne Marie had begun a few minutes before became a slow and steady wail. I raised my head. I watched Mrs. Bradshill as she turned the key in the door. She was now only a silhouette against the burnt-orange backdrop.

I slipped the money into the bank bag in preparation for its deposit and felt a deep sadness come over me. It was as though a piece of my innocence had been taken, both from the reality of Anne Marie's non-existent sister and from the fact that her life had been so torn apart (literally) today. I knew I had a warm house to go home to, friends from school, something I would someday do with my life, but for the moment, standing there in the fading rays of the sun, there was only Mrs. Bradshill moving unhurriedly up the aisle and Anne Marie's wailing—a slow, painful, wordless pleading for something.

As Mrs. Bradshill came closer to the back of the store, the sun moved lower in the firmament, and Anne Marie's cry crescendoed to a painful volume, a gut-wrenching expression of regret and fear, and it continued long after the sky was dark and into the night.

SUMMER MUSIC

The Emperor of Japan died today. Even more shocking was the revelation that he committed suicide. Richard had been the one to see the body first. Both he and Carmella had sensed that something was wrong as they sat on the terrace overlooking the green oasis which was their backyard in Connecticut, but it was Richard who had spotted something out of the corner of his eye. For a second he tried to make sense out of the object without turning his head to see exactly what it was. Before the moment was over he knew what lay in store, for there, nestled in plain view between the geraniums which sat smugly in their stone planters, was the corpse. It lay prone on the sloping green lawn, glistening in the noonday sun.

Richard had jumped up in mid-sentence. His wife, Carmella, didn't understand at first what the problem was. But then she saw the look on his face and knew that bad news was coming. Richard had leapt off the terrace toward the body, hoping that he might perform some sort of resuscitation, but as he neared the corpse, the fact that the Emperor had been dead for some time became painfully evident. A lone fly buzzed at the corner of the Japanese carp's eye, and its golden scales were beginning to show a bluish color. Already the body was beginning to bloat.

"That was a seventy-dollar fish," said Carmella as she stood still on the terrace with hands on hips.

"Well, fish have been known to jump out of the water, usually looking for more water, or maybe just tired of living," said Richard. He looked up at his wife and thought about how long they had been together. After twelve years of marriage she was still as beautiful as ever with her red hair, her freckled shoulders and lithe arms, her athletic thighs and the cute tight walking shorts she always wore when they had coffee on the terrace. "What a pity," he thought, "that we no longer have sex." And they hadn't for the past seven or eight years. That didn't mean they didn't love each other. If anything, their love had seemed to grow stronger over the years. And Carmella still loved him just as much as he loved her. She had a right to. There was plenty there to love.

Richard was six foot four of muscle, with well-developed calves and forearms, and a head of thick black hair. She marveled at the mat of fur on his chest which protruded from the neckline of his Brooks Brothers sport shirt as he stood there looking up at her, helpless as a five-year-old who's just lost his ice cream cone. That was one of the things she liked most about him—the fact that he appeared to be the very model of male virility, yet was capable of being a child at the same time.

She thought about how they still had what could be called a romantic relationship. They still slept together, still laughed at the same things, gave each other attention during the day, and rarely fought, but their sex life was nonexistent. She and Richard had spoken about it, and agreed that they could have their outside sexual outlets. The rule was that neither was to know.

Richard bent down to gently pick up the fish with his strong tanned hands. A fine dusting of hair covered their backs and ran down along his fingers. "He looks like he's been dead for some time," he said, marveling at the now-quite-stiff fish which lay lifeless in his meaty paws. "There's no sign that a raccoon pulled him out, or a heron or gull. My guess is that he just decided he didn't like it in there anymore," and he gestured to the built-up pond which nestled into the embankment between the terrace and the house. "He must have thrown himself out of the water, over the edge and onto the terrace. Since there's no railing on the terrace he probably just flopped around until he went over the edge and onto the grass."

"Oh, Richard," she said, showing more than a modicum of disgust, "don't give me all the details." Then she turned and leaned against the outer rim of the pond which was waist-high, next to the terrace.

Richard had built the pond so that the top was level with the highest point of the slope, and the bottom was a good three feet high, settling onto the beginning of the flagstone patio he had installed himself. He had built the terrace over the summer and both he and Carmella enjoyed being outside during the Connecticut summer days as much as possible, taking full advantage of the prolific green foliage and privacy that surrounded their backyard.

From the terrace they had a view of the woodlands in back of their property; a stream ran through it and there were mounds of azaleas and rhododendrons which Richard had planted last year. And the wildlife was plentiful too—deer, raccoons, possums, and a family of ducks which made a pilgrimage several times a day up to the terrace to receive their doled-out quota of chicken scratch. For Richard and Carmella, summer was their favorite time, especially since the Connecticut winters could be brutal and long. They both liked the hum of the insects, the fact that there was always something blooming, the unplanned visits by woodland creatures, the soft squeak of the bats at dusk. To them it was a type of music. Even the occasional splash of one of the fish in the pond had its charm. But one of those splashes had turned lethal—Richard's prize Japanese koi was now dead.

He remembered the first time he had seen the Emperor at a store downtown that specialized in pond fish. He had never seen anything so beautiful. Most koi were a reddish color, or calico, or had white markings. But this fish was actually gold. There was not a speck of red or white or black to be found on it. Not even in the books on koi that Richard had bought had he seen a fish this exact color. He knew immediately that he had to have it, and without asking the price instructed the store clerk to procure it for him. Not even the cost fazed Richard, and it had been a joy for the past two weeks to point out the unusual fish to neighbors and friends who were over for barbeques or the Fourth of July. "He's called the Emperor," Richard told them, but when they questioned him about the origin of the name, he would just look confused, unable to answer. "Don't know," he would respond. "Just seemed to fit."

"Why would he do it? Jump out like that?" Carmella was asking. She had moved over to the center of the terrace where Richard was standing, holding the fish with an almost religious reverence. Richard shrugged. "Maybe he was just depressed," he said with a seriousness that Carmella had never heard before, and then he lay the body prostrate on the edge of the rock wall surrounding the pond. He peered into the black-green water at the other fish which were still swimming quite contentedly among the lily pads and seaweed he had procured for them. They all seemed fine. Nothing unusual had taken place the days prior to the demise of the Emperor. All the fish appeared to get along, and at one point, the Emperor and another new carp which Richard had purchased at the same time, Balthazar, seemed to be hitting it off, playing a continuous game of "bumper fish." Bumper fish was the name that he and Carmella had given to the interplay that went on between two fish who were mating. One seemed to chase the other around, constantly bumping into the back end of the other one. It was then that they had discovered that the Emperor was actually a female, but because of the way the name stuck to the fish, nothing was done about changing it.

"What are we going to do with him? Her?" Carmella asked. She was thinking how she had kidded Richard about the fact that he had obviously mistaken the fish for male. How were you supposed to tell, anyway?

"We could bury him with the others or I could just put him, or her, in the stream in back and let him float away. Let her float away."

"I kinda go for the stream," said Carmella. "Besides, we haven't had her that long and it wouldn't seem right to bury her with the others." She was thinking about the other family pets that she and Richard had owned over the years. Since there were no children, and didn't appear there ever would be, the two of them were constantly buying small lizards, goldfish, and parakeets from the local pet shop. And not having children, they became extremely attached to these creatures. Then, when the animals went on to bigger and better things, both she and Richard suffered immeasurably. Richard recalled how traumatized Carmella had been by the death of "Playdoh and Socrates," two anoles they had purchased in Manhattan before their move to the country two years ago. First Socrates had died (he was three years old—old by lizard standards) and then Playdoh had succumbed after several months of depression.

The remaining lizard had sat glumly on the stick, high above the water dish, and peered for hours at the sphagnum moss area Socrates had been on when he drew his last breath.

Now, in suburbia, when the couple's pets died, they found a shady, pine-needle-covered location near the side door to the house, and gently moving the hostas and ferns aside, had laid to rest some of their fondest memories. Two lizards, a parakeet, and a goldfish named Dizzy (he had enormous air sacs on each side of his face causing him to resemble the trumpet player, Dizzy Gillespie) were buried there, along with a small field mouse which had appeared like clockwork at the back door several months in a row, waiting for the handout that Richard would give him. So it didn't seem fitting to bury the Emperor in that location. After all, they had only had her for two weeks, not nearly long enough to merit burial in such sacred ground.

"The stream it is," said Richard. Carmella moved next to him, putting one of her slim, braceleted arms around his firm waist. He returned the gesture and they both stood there for a moment looking down at the dead carp. Richard thought how lucky he was to have Carmella as a wife, albeit one he wasn't sexually active with. He really couldn't complain—he had what some men might call an ideal set-up: He was allowed to go out and have his affairs with the women of his choice as long as he didn't bring them home. That meant that Carmella didn't want to hear about them. It wasn't that she was in denial—they had agreed on the arrangement—but rather that she just didn't want to face the reality of the situation on a regular basis. And she couldn't complain either. Here she was in a large house, with all the comforts she could want, with an attractive, understanding man as her husband. He was a good provider. He was the love of her life, and now he was her best friend.

Of course she wanted more. She would have liked to have what she perceived other women had. But she was smart enough to know that the key word was "perception," for deep down she suspected that many marriages had their own set of rules either spoken or unspoken, similar to hers and Richard's. She knew there were marriages like hers that perpetuated the pretense that the couples were faithful, while all along each one had affairs. In some relationships, there were huge fights, breakups, and divorces, all because someone found out about a minor infidelity, when the problem could easily have been solved by an open relationship. She couldn't live with the fighting and broken home, and so one day, after realizing that this was the exact direction they were headed, she and Richard had come to an agreement.

It had been so easy, really. Neither one of them had thought it would be, and they had both spent hours privately agonizing about the situation, only to be relieved when one evening over dinner Richard had said quite calmly, casually, and without any malice, "What do you think about us having sex with other people?" If someone had told her that she would respond with as much nonchalance as he had by that posed question, she would have suggested that they seek professional help, but when it happened, Richard's tone and manner had been so unemotional, so matter-of-fact—as if he were proposing a new line of pipe fitting for one of his clients—that she found herself responding with equal temperance.

"That would be all right with me," she had found herself saying before taking another bite of the Roquefort-laden salad which was poised at the end of her fork, "but I think we need to discuss it, along with some ground rules." It had seemed like a hallucination at the time, as if what they were discussing wasn't real, but as they pursued it, she became more and more aware of the ramifications the proposed situation might present. Strangely, neither she nor Richard felt threatened initially. She hadn't expected him to—wasn't that what men really wanted anyway? Wasn't she supposed to be the one who held the nest together, who responded like an angry gull at some intruder trying to take her security away? Wasn't she supposed to want only one person? It was almost an axiom that men wanted more than one partner, while women were supposed to want the security and companionship of one mate. At least that's how she had been educated by society.

But it was different now. She was secure in her relationship with Richard and didn't feel threatened. That was some of it, but there was something else. Forget the fact that people around them might find out. Forget the fact that they might be viewed as immoral. She was long past that, and hadn't the world learned yet that morality and piety were just a pretense for those who did worse things than the rest of us? But she knew the truth: The ones who were really upstanding and proper were the ones who never opened their mouths about being so. And she wondered if Richard felt similarly; wondered if he had found a common ground that, while it worked for both of them on the surface, was really part of a totally different quest.

Richard had of course been open to the idea. He had been the one to bring it up, but now as he stood there next to her on the terrace, looking over the pond he had built, the home they had made together, he felt a slight tinge of remorse for the decision they had made. Perhaps it would have been better for him to go about his business and be unfaithful, never telling Carmella about the infidelities. It was, after all, quite possible for him to have gotten away with it—the combination of his work schedule, society's parameters, and most women's desire not to know, could have worked wonders for his predicament. Still, he would have felt enormous guilt, and he truly did love his wife—he just didn't want to sleep with her.

But now there was the nagging thought that she might be doing exactly the same thing he was contemplating. They had talked about this open relationship, and he thought he had covered every angle. The truth was, he didn't think Carmella was capable of cheating on him. In a way it wasn't really cheating as they had agreed to the terms. And he thought that if he gave her the option it would be like telling a child, "Yes, you're free to stay up as late as you want to," knowing or hoping that the youngster would fall asleep anyway before twelve. He thought that if Carmella knew she could always have something outside the relationship, she wouldn't really act on it.

"I should go put him in the stream," Richard said, looking down at the poor sad fish—wide-eyed with mouth slightly askew—and wondering exactly where he would be with his wife in five years.

"Want me to go with you?" she asked. Neither of them bothered to look at the other.

"No, I'd rather do it myself. Think it would be better that way."

"That's fine," she said wistfully, "I'd rather not say good-by to him, to *her*, down there anyway. Isn't that muskrat still down there, by the bamboo?"

"I saw him yesterday, chewing a stalk of it and then dragging it into his lair. I think he's got a Mrs. Muskrat now," he said and gently squeezed her arm with his free hand as he looked into her eyes. "Soon, maybe they'll have little muskrats running around."

"You don't think he could have gotten the Emperor out of the pond?" she asked, turning her body to him.

"No. Like I told you, there isn't a mark on him," and with that he turned the fish over to show her. She peered down at it, as if it were a science experiment and Richard was her boyfriend in seventh grade. For a moment she felt as connected to him as she had when they first met. For a brief second there was a magical sense one feels when one doesn't yet know who this person is, when the journey of a relationship is about to be embarked on, yet one feels the certainty that this must be the person the universe has been saving for this specific purpose. The freshness of the thing; the fact that there is so much to learn about the person; the trust you have in them—all of this came to mind. But then it evaporated just as quickly as it had come.

"Besides," he went on, "that muskrat has all the fish he can handle in that stream."

"Well, why don't you do whatever it is you have to do and I'll go inside and get dinner started," she said as she slid out of his grasp. He nodded at the fish. As he made his way down to the stream, his well-worn Topsiders mashed footprints into the tall wet grass. Kneeling down near the edge of the rippling water, he leaned over as far as he could without falling in, and bracing himself on a large rock which protruded out slightly into the brook, lowered the fish into the running water.

High above the downward-sloping property, from the kitchen window, Carmella could see Richard. She had seen him lope his way jockishly down the yard, his long shirttail hanging down in back, his loose shorts swinging around his muscular legs, one arm jerkily bouncing while the other remained still, holding his precious cargo. She had seen him kneel at the bank and brace himself on the rock. It seemed that she could even hear the rush of the water and smell the freshness of the stream. It seemed as if she were right next to him, helping him to lower the body of the Emperor into the water. But she wasn't. She was standing at the window in the kitchen of her home, their home, watching the man she loved sink the body of what had once been a living, breathing, thing into the cool summer water.

As soon as the fish was released into the stream, it seemed to sink and hesitate for a moment. Then it bobbed to the surface and wobbled toward the small rapids. It gently bounced over the smooth moss-covered stones: a small boat; a toy of some child; an object which had always been inanimate and wooden. For a moment it was again hidden from view, pulled underneath by the swirling water of the miniature rapids. Then it surfaced from the roiling water, buoyantly ascending to greet the air like some stiff vegetable rising from the bottom of a boiling pot on a stove.

Once over the rapids it seemed to pick up speed and right itself. It now looked as if it were alive, and indeed, watching from the window, Carmella felt that moment of hope which said that the fish had only been stunned; that the natural water from the stream had somehow revived it and it was now swimming away. But she knew that it was only an illusion of the fast-moving current, and as she watched her husband stand by the stream looking after the koi, she felt something slip away from her. She wasn't sure where she was going. She wasn't even sure what the feeling was. She stood at the window for the longest time, watching what was now a speck of gold bob and weave its way downstream. She watched it until she could see it no more, and then she watched for a good five minutes, just to be sure she was there when it disappeared from sight.

THE DIAPHANOUS LEAVES OF THE ALOCASIA

Cassandra picked at the solitary walnut. It lay forlorn and desolate atop the single slice of her grandmother's fruitcake, prostrate before her on this dreary November late afternoon. The walnut, along with the fruitcake, Cassandra, and a rather eclectic assortment of family members, all sat around the ornately carved dining room table in the cavernous Garden District home. The house, situated in the middle of New Orleans's most prestigious neighborhood, had been in the family for three generations. It was full of soft-ticking clocks and solemn family portraits whose faces and hard stares looked down on plush orientals and over-carved pieces of mahogany.

Slumped to one side at the table, Cassandra went unnoticed by the other family members as she deftly pried the nut free from its doughy prison. To her it was a mastodon in a tar pit; a half brain from an operation she had just performed on a patient; a hubcap from a roaring-by roadster in the 1920s, flung into the gutter barely missing her delicate, silk-stocking clad ankles.

"No," she thought, "I will not become Walter Mitty, just because these relatives of mine are driving me to distraction. Besides, this is the 1990s, not the 1920s, and they probably didn't even *have* mastodons in New Orleans." She chased the walnut around with her grandmother's silver, using one lazy, overly-white limp arm to perform the action. Her head rested sideways atop the other arm like a Brancusi sculpture. Both limbs showed pink and goosepimply like that of the fifteen-year-old girl she was. Convinced at this minute that all of life must have passed her by, Cassandra sank into her depression full force. In her mind she had a lot to be depressed about: Not only the turmoil and drain of the Thanksgiving season (wasn't fruitcake supposed to be for Christmas?), but the vacuous yet splendiferous inanity of her mother and father. Then there were the elderly moments of her grandmother and the penitent aspects of several cousins—both first and second—all of which seemed to be tormenting her, if not literally, then psychically, by their non-verbal insinuations that she attend church with them tomorrow. They stared at her from across an ocean of white tablecloth that was tradition. But no matter how much their faces attempted intimidation, Cassandra would have none of it. She just didn't fit in anymore—anywhere. She felt suffocation taking over; bringing down a veil.

Even this house—her grandmother's house—was a domicile of rooms upon rooms in which it was always night. Rooms which, because of their gloom-colored walls, pompous furniture, exotic wood wainscoting, and heavy draperies, absorbed what light and life infiltrated these chambers, like giant emotional living sponges at the bottom of some underwater cave.

Occasionally a ribbon of sun would filter down into the family (a new birth; someone's wedding; good news about the cancer cells in Uncle Malamar's prostate) only to be sucked into the woodwork, ticking clocks, and dusty Meissens which littered the place. She longed to escape, if not to some other planet, then at least back to her parents' house, several blocks Uptown. But her grandmother had insisted that Thanksgiving be held at the family home this year, and so here she was, amid the half-known relatives, resplendent with their odd criticisms and their subtle ways of disapproving.

Her grandmother alone was a piece of work—the matriarch wasn't exactly the warmest person. The old woman's mind had started to resemble one of the lace doilies she had lying around—full of holes, some intentional, some not—yellowing and limp so that no amount of bleach or starch could have repaired the problem. The old woman was tired. After all, she had been a parent to Cassandra's mother and that would have exhausted anyone. And it seemed fitting to Cassandra that her mother had begun to resemble the grandmother now. The mother had even acknowledged it, looking into her vanity mirror night after night to see the lines forming on her forehead, the shifting of fat deposits, the skin sagging in places she hadn't thought about. Wrinkles appeared like giant gullies after a lifetime of pushing and pulling. "Doug, do you think I'm looking old?" she would ask the sullen husband, Cassandra's father, suddenly realizing all of the things she hadn't yet done with her life and hoping that at least a few could be attempted before another crease crept up to join the others—creases and lines which had gathered next to her wide green eyes like morbid passersby, eager to catch a glimpse of some bad accident or injured victim. Cassandra's relationship with her mother wasn't much of an issue. In fact, it had pretty much been nonexistent, and this, along with the fact that Cassandra's father could barely remember his child's name, was what she considered the only saving grace of the household. At least she was left somewhat alone. In her mind she just didn't fit in with anyone, but especially with her mother and father, and so this blatant ignorance of her existence actually served as a balm rather than some grave irritation. She wondered if they expected her eventually to be like them with their wainscoting and doilies, and if not with those exact attributes, then with modern facsimiles representative thereof. She thought about this as she moved the solitary nut about the hand-painted rim of the dessert plate. To her there was only one saving grace about this city, only one thing which allowed her to escape, and it was a world more interesting than any she had seen on trips to Mexico or Europe or the Orient—it was a land called the French Quarter.

At least by living in New Orleans, Cassandra could escape to the Quarter, that marvelous fetid and dank place where drinking and sex were as much a part of the fabric—at least on Bourbon Street—as they had been in a wild, wild west saloon a hundred years ago. In the Quarter no one questioned her age, her background, or anything else about her. If anything, the oily businessmen eyed her with more than a modicum of lust and the surly bartenders marked her as tourist bait for their business. And even *that* was better than staying at her grandmother's house in the Garden District, having to feign pleasure in one more mouthful of cornbread stuffing or jellied cranberry sauce. Thank God, they at least lived *in* New Orleans and not a small town like some of the cousins.

She remembered once visiting her cousin Irma in Woodville, Mississippi. While it was a quaint enough town, it was not the place for a teenager. Making artillery punch and playing Monopoly proved to be only mildly entertaining, and everyone went to bed at nine-thirty under a moonlit sky and mosquito netting. It was an experiment that Cassandra didn't want to repeat. Evidently, some of the aunts and uncles didn't find life outside New Orleans very exciting either, because they usually jumped at the chance to come into the city to celebrate Thanksgiving, staying on for several days in order to gamble or scour the antique shops on Magazine Street.

After what seemed like interminable conversation about cousin Larry's new oil refinery job and whether or not her father was going to take the Cranford case (he was a lawyer—one of the most influential in New Orleans), all of the coffee was exhausted and the relatives started to trickle out of the Victorian behemoth that was the family home, returning to their own houses or respective hotels. Whether returning home or to the Sheraton or Monteleone, Cassandra knew they would probably fall fast asleep, missing the action that the Crescent City had to offer. "What a dull bunch of broods," she thought as her mother and father made their way down the wooden front steps of her grandmother's house, then into the soft air-conditioned confines of the Cadillac, pulling Cassandra behind them like some worn-out child's toy on wheels.

As soon as she found herself in the middle of her own bedroom in her parent's home, Cassandra tore off the overly frilly dress she had been forced to wear. It was something that amazed her about New Orleans. While it was a cosmopolitan city, it held some values near and dear to its heart, one of them being the requirement that relatives still dress for special occasions and family gatherings—at least the relatives with money and breeding. Even in other cities such as Los Angeles and Denver, most children weren't required to wear anything more than jeans and a clean shirt. Not in New Orleans.

As she lay on her bed waiting for her parents to cease fighting and enter their truce-calling dream world, she thought about her life. It seemed to her to have an ephemeral quality, like those one-day insects which hovered over the muddy Mississippi's banks. She realized the analogy wasn't exact, but still, she couldn't help but feel everything was passing her by. Life was one big Mardi Gras parade and she was at home sick with the flu.

Finally she perceived her parents to be asleep. Not that it really mattered, for it seemed to Cassandra that her lack of attention and sensitivity to the details of remaining quiet was the one thing that saved her from getting caught. It was always when she tried hardest not to make a sound that her mother and father were out of bed faster than they would have been had the house been ablaze. If she were careless and walked about with a regular cadence, almost slamming doors, her parents would snooze soundly through the entire process. It seemed to her at the time a representation of life itself. She had been taught to be courteous, careful, wise, cautious, and all the other attributes which genteel families thought beneficial to a young lady of her social standing, but in reality she seemed to fare better when she was unorthodox and slightly rude. Perhaps the rest of the world only understood *their* way of communicating and simply looked aghast at anything that was different. Manners, nowadays, seemed to be frowned upon by society outside of a few well-decorated Uptown homes.

During this last thought process she had managed to put on a pair of loose-fitting baggy blue jeans and an old sweatshirt. It was getting chilly this time of year, even in tropical New Orleans. Her hair pulled back, and just a hint of eyeliner and rouge on her face, she made her way from the hallway to the vertiginous staircase with the attitude of one who seeks the kitchen for a midnight snack—eager to find what leftovers have been stored away, but not totally ecstatic since it is the stomach defining the course of action and not the head. Not that she would have cared if she were caught. She would have just sulked and then tried again later. Besides, it was always easier to exit via the kitchen door where you could more easily manipulate the burglar alarm, and if her parents did hear her tumbling about, they would probably make the food connection and go back to sleep.

Soon she was free on the fresh wet lawn, the hem of her jeans becoming soaked with dew from the overachieving monkey grass which grew in profusion alongside the house, reaching out to caress her ankles like some deviant old man trying to cop a feel in a shoe store. As she padded her way down the ancient concrete walk which led to the side gate, a small rodent skittered in front of her and hid underneath an azalea. She sucked in her breath and kept walking. The only sound now was the heavy fabric of insect noises and the occasional electric hum of a streetlight. It was barely a few blocks to the streetcar on St. Charles which would take her to another planet entirely—Bourbon Street. As she stretched the sleeves of her sweatshirt downward so that they covered her hands, she noticed the moist Gulf air as it swirled around the lazy median which is the grassy middle section of New Orleans's second most famous street. Bastions of old homes stood silent with dark windows on St. Charles. Live oaks bent down as if to tell her a secret, then whispered nothing as if the entire charade had been played out to make her ill at ease. Shoots of ginger splayed themselves against the excessive whiteness of a columned house, and passing headlights spun ghost tales in the settled-glass windows of some of the city's most impressive mansions.

It seemed she waited forever for the streetcar, teetering on the edge of the curb, listening to the sounds the solitary vehicles made at this time of night. Eventually the gray-green pod-car plodded toward her, opening its doors even more slowly than usual to admit her when it finally eased to a halt. She received a suspicious look from the driver. Shrugging it off, she sat down a few rows from the back. This was New Orleans, and who was the driver to question a fifteen-year-old girl out for a night on the town? Hadn't he himself probably had a fifteen-year-old at one time in the back of one of the strip clubs on Bourbon Street? She imagined the man sticking his unctuous tongue into the ear of some nascent and squealing adolescent as he balanced a gin and tonic in one hand and squeezed the teenager's waist with the other. The thought made her shudder, and as she felt his eyes walk all over her in his mirror, she settled further down into the wooden bench.

As the car lurched forward she pointed her attention to the passing scene. The boxed view provided her with snippets of life on St. Charles, even at that late hour. As they neared the busier parts of the street—nearer the business district—they passed an array of New Orleans Garden District nightlife: fancily dressed couples after an evening of dining and dancing; what looked like the remnants of a wedding party; drunks of assorted shapes and sizes; and even what appeared to be a carjacking. Finally they were approaching the turnaround for the line, near Canal Street. Only a minute more and she would be free from her family and The District—free to be anyone she wanted.

As she descended the steps of the car, she felt the anticipation that one reserves for airplane trips and opening nights at the theatre. It seemed that the light to cross Canal Street stayed red forever, and even at this hour there was no way of crossing without its assistance as the town in this section, at this time of night, was buzzing. "Amazing," she thought, "that on Thanksgiving night this place would be crowded with people searching for a good time." But then, she was there for the very same reason.

Finally she was on Bourbon Street. Walking the brick surface, she felt herself akin to a prisoner of war returning home after a long absence. She wanted to kiss the ground. The decaying doorways with their dripping air conditioners overhead (even in cool weather) welcomed her, and further down, toward Esplanade, the sounds of revelry and seditious behavior lured her like some magic thread tied to her wrist. It was always like this, as if you had lost your free will and were now subjected to the magic, the evil, the gaiety that ran like a current through these bricks and houses and whores and debauchery and drinking masses, rather than your intended will. The Quarter was a thing in itself, a being all its own with rules and fancies and a history like no other place. Even New York could not compare in Cassandra's mind. New York, with its bevy of worn-out businessmen, its gridlock of streets, its vertical expanses. New Orleans, and most specifically the French Quarter, was different. It was Paris and San Juan and Key West all rolled into one. And it was all located within several square blocks.

The hour was late. Cassandra made her way into one of the open-air bars and sauntered up to the rail. She mouthed the word "beer" knowing that she could not compete with the high-decibel rock band which was performing in one corner of the room. Transaction complete, she made her way around the space. She had done this several times before—enough times to know her way around—and tonight she felt like pushing the envelope. But not here. She wanted something more high caliber—some new experience, something off the beaten path. As the band finished one of its sets, she caught the eye of what appeared to be a college freshman, standing alone. Being the precocious girl of fifteen that she was, she sauntered over toward him, studying him like a bug under glass. After only a few minutes he moved away, unable to discern her intentions. Without finishing her beer (it had been so easy to procure that it wasn't considered the teenage equivalent of gold normally associated with outings such as this), she left the bar, letting her body fall from the doorway and down the sidewalk with a loopy, carefree gait. As she wove her way down Bourbon Street, dodging slatternly college men, over-painted housewives, and assorted girls her own age (most bent at a perfect right angle, expectantly awaiting their stomach's retribution for a night of mixing beer and wine with Hurricanes—that infamous New Orleans drink), she became almost oblivious to the carnival-like surroundings. It was strange. She had come to the French Quarter expressly for this purpose, of being in the exact center of things, and yet she found herself moving away from the noise, the lights, the smells which rose around her like some giant laughing clown whose intentions aren't totally honorable or without malice.

Turning onto one of the streets which ran across Bourbon like a set of tire tracks, she headed for Preservation Hall—that bastion of real-time jazz located in a falling-down, tattered shell of a building. She was actually able to approach the front door on this night because of the holiday, and found it to be more sparsely populated than she had ever known. Still, there were the die-hard jazz junkies, tourists, and the occasional nodding, aged jazz musician in the corner. At least the band wasn't playing "Saints." But they were playing something equally as lively. As she stood in the shadows watching the show, she noticed how alarmingly small the space was.

Because of the cramped quarters, the sounds of the pealing clarinet and thumping bass reverberated off the old walls and bounced around the room. She became aware that her face and lips were vibrating, the way they did when you were a child at Halloween and you pressed your mouth to a cheap dime store mask. After a while, with your face sweating and feeling claustrophobic, you opted for the mask's removal and weathered the search for candy and amusement without any disguise at all.

So it was with her Preservation Hall experience. She wasn't really in the mood for jazz anyway, and as she stepped down onto St. Peter Street and headed over to Royal she became aware that her inhibitions (what few she had) had dropped away from her, and that her emotional mask had been discarded as well.

While Bourbon Street was a raucous carnival, a veritable heroin-filled vein in the arm of a good-natured but somewhat worn and morphine-addicted dowager, the side streets of the Quarter were deserted and ominous. Just six feet to the right or left of Bourbon the party seemed to stop with only the occasional drunk or shady character lurking within a doorway, and as Cassandra watched the gaudy, lighted street from a distance now, she became aware of its flowing mass of people. It resembled to her the mighty Mississippi, only made of people and lights, ebbing and flowing between Canal and Esplanade. She hurried quickly toward the river, toward Royal Street where shop after shop of antiques provided a feast for the eye even at night with their well-lighted windows, crammed full of ormolu candelabra, crystal-heavy chandeliers, and patina-laden objets d'art.

It was always the same, this effect the shop windows had on her. The opulent wares seemed to beckon even though the doors had been shut for hours. Royal Street was a world away from Bourbon with only the lost college freshman, the two lovers who wanted to be alone, or the musician who thought he could do better on a quieter street. As she strode beside the decadent windows, something caught her attention. It wasn't so much a thing of beauty or opulence as a feeling that drew her to the window. It was the shape, the commanding presence of the thing, the ominous foreboding quality that it gave off. In the back-lit window of one of the shops stood a dark, bronze angel, maybe three feet high. Its wings stretched upward triumphantly while one hand rested on its hip and another grasped a sword which appeared to be stuck in the bronze earth at its feet. It was majestic and terrifying as it defied the other bronzes, the silver cigarette cases, and the enamelware vases that littered around it. Hanging above it, like giant rain drops before their Armageddon-like fall downward to earth, were thousands of crystal pendants, their refracting qualities seemingly suspended in mid-air as they hovered just below the brass chandeliers which held them aloft. The effect was at once both magical and evil.

Cassandra hurried down Royal, the street becoming more and more deserted as she neared Esplanade. Bourbon and Royal were as different as night and day, and as she let her mind slip further and further from the unholy tentacles of the former street and into the more sedate latter, preparing to venture in the direction of the French Market, she became aware of a sound. At first she thought it might be the sultry air from the Mississippi playing acoustic tricks with the ancient and crumbling building façades, or perhaps a few notes which had escaped the bawdy street a few blocks over from some horizontal clarinet or vertical trumpet. But then she listened, and the sound seemed to come into focus. It was someone singing. Softly.

Ordinarily she wouldn't have given it much thought, but the quality this singing had was something altogether different. And it seemed to be emanating from one of the narrow passageways which led from the street to a hidden courtyard. She stopped as a dog might—as if to analyze the air.

The notes were floating toward her through a dark, narrow carriageway which connected one of New Orleans's inner courtyards with the world of the street. As she leaned into the sooty wrought-iron gate which—like so many in the Quarter, performed the purpose of keeping out nosy tourists—it gave way slightly and opened. She looked around. The squeak that the old bars emitted hadn't attracted any attention. Besides, the street was empty and quiet except for one or two people crossing Toulouse several blocks away, their shadowy figures leaning into the night as if escaping some irate pirate ghost. Having been in the Quarter many times, not only by herself, but with her parents, Cassandra knew of the courtyards and these iron gates which stood between the lush tropical gardens and throngs of visiting tourists on the sidewalk. Never before had she seen anyone enter or exit these gates, much less happen upon one which was unlocked.

Her curiosity got the better of her. Not a sound escaped now as she pushed on the dull, rusted gate, easing her way into the low tunnel that led to the inner patio. The temperature seemed to drop a good five or six degrees just inside the building, even though the bars of the gate were wide enough to admit the air from the street. As she slowly made her way to the sound of the voice, she became aware of rusted, sagging pipes overhead, the layers of dust on everything, the peeling lead paint which clung to the two-hundred-year-old bricks like lichen. Nearing the opening to the courtyard, she became aware that there was someone standing to the rear of the open space, in front of a raised flowerbed. The profusion of thick foliage surrounding Cassandra seemed to take on an animated quality, and she felt herself almost float into the center of this miniature jungle. Of all the courtyards or pictures of such that she'd seen in books on New Orleans, this one appeared to be the most lush. Then the figure standing at the rear of the courtyard noticed her for the first time, and Cassandra noticed that the figure now seemed to become visually separated from a verdant thicket of leaves which surrounded a small stone fountain. A moss-covered cherub gently poured out the lackadaisical contents from its jug, filling the inner space with the soft sound of water upon water, its languid, soothing murmurs helping to draw the young girl further into the green sanctuary of night.

"There you are," said the rather portly outline of a woman holding a candle. Her voice was calm as if she had been expecting Cassandra. Now the picture was coming into focus more clearly. She was a middle-aged woman, probably in her forties, dressed in a rather loose-fitting shift and tight shorts. She was barefoot. Cassandra couldn't make out the color of the woman's clothes. In fact, the whole scene seemed to have a gray-green colorless aspect, except for the red mesh-covered candle which the woman was holding—a cast-off from some outdoor café on one of the Quarter's side streets. It threw a ghostly glow onto the giant leaves of elephant ears and palmettos, which returned the gesture by pitching their long oval shadows onto the brick and stucco planes of the surrounding house. Walls loomed upwards—witches at some ritualistic meeting, huddled closely together for warmth with O-mouths and blank, soulless eyes held in check by cypress shutters—and the blue-black sky holding a lopsided square high above the scene, emitting only a star or two for reference.

Suddenly, one of the solitary stars shot silently down to earth—only for a second—and then disappeared. Life seemed suspended, as if by some pernicious magician's hand, held by an invisible thread. Then things began to move again, and the prestidigitation of the moment melted back into the previous mood of the evening with its almost salacious vegetation and night air resplendent with the thick scent of wet stone. Within the fountain a small goldfish jumped slightly, causing the thicket of water hyacinths which covered virtually the entire surface of the pool to move gently about like passengers in some crowded elevator making space for a new arrival who carried too many packages.

Cassandra approached the woman. She felt as if she were supposed to know her. At least she didn't feel afraid. After all, she thought, it must be the woman's house, her courtyard, her candle, her banana trees, her fountain. The woman motioned to Cassandra with one hand to come closer. Cassandra felt herself obeying, though she wasn't sure why. When she was three feet from the figure, she began to make sense of the entire scene. At the overweight woman's feet (complete with red-chipped toenail polish and a large corn) was the frail and extremely stiff body of a cat. Not just any cat though, as it was malnourished and had a sad, eerie quality about it. Enormous patches of fur were missing, and the left side of its face (the one facing Cassandra) was almost entirely gone. Cassandra looked up at the woman who was now holding the candle just below her own face. Though not for the purpose of creating a visage to terrify Cassandra, the woman nevertheless proceeded to that exact result.

The young girl stepped back, looking disturbed, and the woman lowered the candle, setting it down on the stone ledge which sat below the enormous green leaves of one of the many elephant ears that inhabited the courtyard.

"Don't be afraid," the woman said, and extended her fleshy arm in Cassandra's direction. The girl moved toward the woman until she was standing beside her, so close that she felt they might be about to have their picture taken. Again, Cassandra didn't know why she allowed herself to perform this action. It was as if something was taking control of her body and mind, instructing or *allowing* her to follow a certain premeditated path in order to reach a predetermined conclusion.

"I found him on Frenchmen Street, just off Elysian Fields," the woman was saying, never taking her eyes off the dead cat. The flickering flame of the enclosed candle made the shadows jump from side to side. Cassandra could hear bits of conversation and laughter, music and horse hoofs, as sounds filtered over the rooftops, managing to fall into the catacomb-like space she was now in.

"You mean he wasn't your cat?" Cassandra asked as she looked up at the woman. Though she had spoken in a normal tone, the words seemed to be quickly absorbed by the plethora of plants, the humid air, the moment.

"Heavens no, I don't have any pets. I just bury them," the woman said in a soft voice. Cassandra thought how she had never heard a voice such as this. It reverberated as if a dead person were speaking, if they could speak—completely void of anger and hate. As Cassandra's eyes began adjusting to the scene, she made out more details. The woman had dug up huge chunks of earth from around the base of a plant, an enormous elephant ear. Cassandra remembered these plants in her grandmother's garden. What had her grandmother called them? Alocasias? Something like that. In addition to the disturbed earth, several bromeliads had been dislocated and there was a small garden spade resting at the base of the giant rubbery green Alocasia—its enormous fleshy stems coming together in the earth at a point which resembled a massive organic light bulb screwed into the dry brown casing of heavy root, which in turn reached down into the terrain like some breathing animal—phantasmagoric. Then

Cassandra realized that the woman had said, "them," when referring to the cat.

"How many have you buried here?" ventured Cassandra, her voice taking on a hushed, religious quality. It was hard not to follow suit with the lateness of the evening, the candle, the dead feline whose life had obviously been difficult.

The woman looked around at the arching boughs of a crepe myrtle tree, the spiky palmettos, the languid tree fern sheltering itself in the corner. "Lots," she said and took Cassandra's hand and squeezed it. "Strange," thought Cassandra, "how I would allow this woman to take my hand. How I would allow myself to be standing here, in a strange courtyard, with a dead cat." It was as though she had entered a new world when she entered this space, one that allowed her to be someone other than who life, up until this point, had determined her to be. It was as if the moment she moved through the damp stone carriageway, some transformation had taken place, and Cassandra now felt the last of her inhibitions fall away.

Then she found herself saying and doing something even more strange. "Would you mind?" she started to ask the woman, her eyes wide as a small child's. But then she stopped and looked down. The woman squeezed Cassandra's hand and the young girl looked up, now with the courage to finish the request. The fountain continued its repetitive gurgle, filling in the silences.

"Would you mind," she began again, "if I buried him?" Her tone was flat and unemotional, without inflection, as though the voice had come from some part of her other than the normal speaking apparatus she usually employed. It was if she were having some sort of out-of-body experience. She couldn't believe she was asking for this favor—to do this deed, with this cat, near this woman, in this courtyard. It was as if the moment she had entered the small enclosed space, she had changed, and done so in some way other than just temporarily physically or emotionally—as if she had taken on a new personality. It was as if she were a completely different person because she was in the presence of this strange woman. And as she stood there, the question hovering in the air like some unreal and oversized papier-mâché insect, she took in the woman's features. Her flesh was milk-white and solid. Beneath her too-tight shorts, ridges of cellulite flowed down her large thighs. Her arms, too, were overly fleshy and there seemed to be an inordinate amount of skin at her neck. Occasionally a freckle or mole dotted her forearms, her brow, her exposed nape, but other than that the woman seemed almost colorless.

The woman smiled, and it seemed to Cassandra that nothing was said for the longest time. Cassandra feared she had somehow misspoken or offended. Maybe the woman thought she was some lunatic who had wondered in off the street? Maybe she had been slighted because most of the work had already been done—the grave dug, the plant life cleared away.

"You go right ahead, sweetheart," she said, and moved the candle onto the earth directly below the colossal rubbery plates of the elephant ear. The light shone upward making the leaves a brilliant emerald green, allowing the lucent flames and energy of the candle to filter through them and onto the walls of the courtyard with watery, ghost-like results.

Cassandra knelt beside the raised bed. She lifted the body of the animal by the white pillow case on which it was resting. It almost seemed to raise itself up, so light was the corpse, as if its internal organs had been removed. Once it was in position, in the shallow grave below the sway of ferns and impatiens, she carefully filtered the rich black dirt though her fingers and around the feline, being cautious to cover the animal's face and sides with the edges of the pillowcase before burying it completely. She replaced one of the impatiens at its head, and another near the middle of the cat. Carefully, she smoothed the dirt all around the buried animal as if she were putting to rest fears and tribulations she had endured all her short life. As she was finishing, she became aware of the woman standing over her, hands on hips, non-judgmental, overseeing—a mother watching her three-year-old make mud pies.

Cassandra stood up, her knees almost giving way, and as she faced the woman, she felt as though she had known her for longer than just these few minutes in this courtyard in this city which located itself on the bend of the Mississippi River. The woman reached up and brushed a tear from Cassandra's eye.

Neither spoke, and Cassandra felt this must be a dream. She noticed the candle which burned well below the giant leaves of the tropical foliage. The light magically transformed the courtyard as it made its way up through the filaments of green, the rubbery flesh of the plant—the diaphanous leaves of the Alocasia. A second later and it was gone, extinguished by the very woman who had lit it in the first place.

The woman moved slowly toward Cassandra, and when she reached the young girl they both turned and headed down the musty passageway and out onto the street, strolling together as if their movements had been designed by some emerging underling, employed by a theatre that couldn't afford to hire the proper professionals.

"Shouldn't you lock the gate?" asked Cassandra as the woman closed the rusted and patina-laden mechanism with a velvety click.

"How could I?" asked the woman with genuine curiosity.

It was then that Cassandra realized the strangest element of the evening wasn't the burial of a cat in a damp tropical courtyard, in a city that was six feet below sea level, but this: The fact that the woman didn't live at this address. Cassandra was filled with a mixture of shock and elation the way one is when finding out that one's stodgy old-fashioned parents once stole a car or were thrown in jail.

She turned to the woman who was now standing attentively, waiting for some question she knew would be asked of her. It came after a humid pause. "Have you buried many cats in the courtyard, in this particular courtyard?" Cassandra asked.

"A few. I find them here and there, mostly in bad neighborhoods or near the river. Abandoned, lonely animals. Lost souls that nobody wants or that have died a tragic death. Then I look for a gate that someone's left open. Holidays like this are good too. People go away or they're with relatives so there's less chance of someone seeing you."

"How long have you done it? Bury them?"

"About, oh, fourteen years now. At least as far as I can remember."

Now they were walking down Royal Street toward Esplanade—that forgotten sister-street of New Orleans with its dark towering trees and its shuttered windows and cracked sidewalks; a street relegated to spend its life guarding one side of the French Quarter, always keeping its back to the fun and mayhem. The woman seemed to warm toward Cassandra, even more than before. "You know, I always wished I had a girl like you—somebody to keep me company. Maybe then I wouldn't have to go around burying strange animals that I find," and with that the woman gave a small, throaty laugh.

"You don't have any children?" Cassandra asked, looking up at the woman. They had stopped in front of a darkened store window. Dusty, broken Chinese puppets looked down at them, suspended from a metal pipe, and several musical instruments from Africa littered the shop window. A collection of paperweights stretched back from the aged glass to the inside of the shop, looking like some stoic throng of adolescents at a youth rally, waiting for the very instructions of life, transparent but each with a secret locked deep inside its hard shell.

"I had a child once. A baby really. She died when she was only a day old. I had her at home and so my husband was the only one who . . ." but the woman trailed off and seemed to lose herself in remembering. Then she cast a quick glance back at the courtyard—quiet, wistful, concerned. Cassandra looked down at the pavement, then across the street—anything in order to make the woman feel more at ease. She suddenly felt horribly embarrassed about asking this complete stranger if she had ever had children. Cassandra started to speak, but she stopped before the words came from her mouth. Then she looked up into the store window. A multi-jointed Mandarin peered down at her out of black eyes. His hands hung loosely at his sides and he leaned slightly forward on his wire so that his faded, dust-covered cloak of crimson and gold hung freely in front. Then she noticed her reflection as well as that of the street. At first it shocked her. She could see her reflection among the exotica which overflowed back into the shop, but not her companion's. Within a second, myriad things went through her mind, but then she turned and discovered that the woman was actually gone and not just some spirit whose reflection Cassandra couldn't see.

The young girl looked down Royal Street and caught the last glimpse of the woman slowly rounding the corner at Esplanade. Cassandra turned to go, attempting to retrace her steps back to the streetcar—back to the edges of the French Quarter near Canal Street. Oddly, she didn't feel abandoned by the woman. It was as if no good-by were necessary, as if they could communicate at almost any time deemed necessary. True, the departure had been abrupt and unusual, but no more so than the initial meeting earlier that evening.

Once again Cassandra found her way to Bourbon Street with its gaudy atmosphere, which, although somewhat calmer than before, was now offensive to her—out of place and rancid. The street had yet to become the potpourri of Pine-Sol and regurgitated Heineken that it metamorphosed into each early morning, and it seemed to Cassandra that all of the French Quarter's blocks were running together as in some vast, melting, phantasmagoric dream—surreal yet reminiscently fetching at the same time. Stretches of brick and pavement were now giving way to Canal Street, and Canal was giving way to the river, and the tourists, prostitutes, and college students seemed to fade into the gray buildings of a false pre-dawn. Cassandra knew she couldn't handle the streetcar at this hour. She wasn't even sure what hour it was or if the thing ran this late, so she hailed a cab and gave the driver her address.

As the noises and smells of debauchery which make up Bourbon Street receded from her memory, she began to accept the transition back Uptown. A Christmas-tree-shaped deodorizer swung back and forth from the rearview mirror of the cab in rhythm to the faint strains of Zydeco music emanating from the radio. Even though the music was new, it took on an entirely different aura coming out of the red plastic speaker on the dashboard. The car was a 1966 Impala, but the driver and the decade were well into the nineties.

Cassandra asked to be let out on St. Charles Avenue so that the sound of a car door slamming wouldn't arouse suspicion on the quiet side street her family lived on, and with the precision of a burglar, she made her way back into her parents' house.

The next day made itself known through the lace curtains which hung under the heavy draperies of her room. As Cassandra slowly became aware of the world outside her window, she had that feeling you sometimes experience when, awakening late in the day, you sense that you've been cheated out of something—a feeling that the rest of the world was able (up until now) to function without your help—that you weren't really needed.

As she rose, treating the day with the careful sensitivity one reserves for old teacups and small birds, she sensed something different about the light, the air, the very heat from the sun which was streaming in the window. She dressed. Then she walked toward the heavy draperies, tasseled and fringed to reflect the room's reproduced Victorian era. Yesterday she had been like a wasp, flinging itself into the dusty glass panes of the sunroom windows, unable to comprehend that something bigger and more expansive than itself could create an obstacle so invisible yet so efficient. Unable to escape or retrace the route which had brought it here, it was eventually to die among the African violets, wicker furniture, and books on English farmhouses. Then it would be swept up weeks later, along with the skittering dust bunnies and dead fern leaves, hardly noticed by anyone—its only reflective moment the one when the dustpan hovered above the garbage pail before letting it drop rather unceremoniously into oblivion.

But now she felt differently. She was no longer like that desperate insect, waiting for some opening to the outside world. The morning felt different. It was like a newly hatched bird which, having fallen from its nest and the secure comforts of its home, spasmodically waits, its mouth forming a soundless cry, its wings still too wet to be of much help. It waits, knowing that either its mother or some strong pair of gardener's hands, gently encased in moss-stained gloves, will rescue it and replace it to the high lair that is its home, its security, its future.

And as she stared out the window to the garden below, to the aging picket-fenced yard with its lush foliage, she remembered the evening before and the burial of the dead animal. She remembered how, not even realizing it at the time, she had come upon something so wonderful and new and unexpected, that she had been transformed, like light through some velvety leaf in some obscure garden on some dark street, shining upwards, and transforming not only herself, but the very area she inhabited.

She opened the lace draperies and peered into the yard. The sun flowed through the window now with ferocity and lustfulness, and Cassandra felt as if her entire body were translucent, fibrous, and green, as if she were waiting to be born. She stood for a few minutes longer, feeling empowered as one does from sex or caffeine or daydreams. Then she turned, and with this newfound part of herself, this remembering, she moved toward the door, down the hallway, and into the remainder of life.

PRIMORDIAL ANGST

Kiki was struggling now. The body weighed infinitely more than she had expected. As she tightened her stomach muscles and concentrated, trying to force every ounce of strength she had into her arms and legs, she noticed a strange sensation floating up from the depths of her abdomen. Queasiness. She hadn't counted on this part. Preoccupied with moving the body, she had failed to take into account the discharge of blood that the killing had produced. With each heave of the heavy torso, more of the red substance flowed onto the ground. Had she really thought about what the act of killing entailed she probably would have reconsidered. But it had been a crime of passion, taking place in such a quick instant that it was as if someone else were pulling the trigger, feeling the kick of the gun, seeing his body drop with a thud onto the grassy lawn. And now she was left with the aftermath.

She knew that she had to hide the body—get it out of sight before the neighbors saw it and called the police—so now she was pulling with all her power, trying not to notice the volumes of blood which sprang from the chest wound, trying to concentrate on her task. If only she could make it to the woods in back of the house she would be able to sink the corpse into the mire of the wetlands. She knew of a place not far from the footbridge where the land seemed to sink forever—New Jersey swamp that was neither soil nor sand nor humus. That would have to do. No time to dismember him and put the parts into suitcases as she had once seen in a movie.

Finally, after what seemed like an eternity, the body was hauled over the freshly mown lawn, accidentally over two newly planted hostas, and carefully around the new ostrich ferns which she had planted. By grasping his ankles, she had dragged him a good sixty feet before once stopping to rest. "Must be the adrenaline," she thought, as she finally stood upright and wiped her forehead with the back of her hand. The body was now hidden in the knotweed and wild irises which grew at the edge of her property. She sat down for a moment on a tree stump to rest, then immediately caught sight of his large brown eyes staring at her. She hadn't counted on that part. The bastard. Even in death he was a pain in the ass. After walking back to the house to find a shovel, she began the arduous task of removing enough of the muck in the marshy area to conceal his torso, and managed to bury him in the wetlands, heaping great piles of lawn debris and other foliage over the mound just in case some unsuspecting children from the neighboring subdivision came through the woods, looking as they were apt to, for small salamanders and toads that inhabited the area. The entire process of dragging the body, digging the hole, heaving it over the edge, and covering it, took more than three hours.

The deed was now done. All that remained was to wash the blood from the lawn. When she was through, she sat on her patio, wiping her forehead once again with the back of her hand, breathing in the heavy summer New Jersey air. "How strange," she thought, "that the guilt would so quickly be gone after the killing." After all, she had been so tormented by him for the past several days, that now he was gone all she could feel was relief. She tried to turn her attention to something else, anything, in order to get her mind off what she had just done. She looked around the patio area.

"My poor flowers," she murmured to herself, distracted for a moment as she bent over, turning her attention to the edge of her flagstone terrace, surveying the patchy and withered foliage. The tops of the delicate flowers were nipped clean off, as if some garden-hating eighteenth-century Paris mob had taken the pruning shears to them—each a miniature Marie Antoinette. Now her gaze moved to the geraniums, their fuzzy verdant leaves optimistically upturned and welcoming the sun.

"Well," she thought, settling back into the cast-iron metal chair, returning to her latest predicament, "at least I'm safe now. No one can hurt me. The police haven't been out here, so the neighbors must have thought the gunshot was a car backfiring. And no one saw." But as she sat there, she thought about how it had all happened—the rage; the months of antagonism beforehand.

It was two weeks ago, exactly to the day, when she had first seen him. He was tall and muscular; proud with that touch of arrogance that makes one take notice. She had been standing at the kitchen sink, not really thinking about anything in particular, having just gotten off the phone with her husband who was assigned to develop a software solution for a company in Seattle. He would be staying in that city for the next several weeks.

She remembered how she had seen the newcomer in her backyard for the first time and marveled at his appearance. It seemed to overtake her, as though he were courting her subconsciously, as if he was not totally aware of his own prowess. At first she thought he was lost; that he had possibly wandered into her yard from a neighbor's he had been visiting, but she had made her way out onto the landing of the back stairs and he hadn't moved. He had taken her in with his eyes—large, brown, sensitive eyes—which seemed to devour her—look right through her. She felt some primordial urge rise in her. It was as if this feeling had been dormant for hundreds of years and was now coming to the surface, recalling ages ago when instinct ruled and rational thoughts were cast to the wind.

They had stared each other down and then he had simply and quietly walked away. It was at that moment that she had noticed his muscular shoulders, the sinewy part of his torso, the animal way that he moved. But with the action of turning away, she had felt a withdrawal as sure as if a lover had interrupted their relationship with some casual crude gesture—something as simple and insulting as reaching for another beer from the icebox as she tried to tell him about her day at home.

Returning inside, she had reached for the phone to call the neighbor—the one whose yard she had seen him come from. But something had told her to stop. It was as if the secret were theirs alone and any discussion of it would mar the magic of that brief moment when they held each other with only a gaze.

She thought nothing of it for the remainder of that day, but the next morning when she opened the back door with the intention of airing some throw rugs, she saw him again. She knew she should have felt some type of fear, as if she were being stalked, but all she could think of was his intense beauty. In her eyes he was magnificent, god-like, as if some sculptor had created him out of marble. There was an element of magic about him—

his fine features; the proud stance; the overtly sexual and dominating nature he possessed as if he had been given carte blanche by God to travel about the universe.

Then her thoughts turned to her husband. What would he have said? She had a pretty good idea, knowing how the man felt about anything that even momentarily took her attention away from him, and especially about an intruder in their yard. Perhaps then he would understand why she had killed. She would explain to him how the whole thing had happened; how the meeting had started out innocently enough; how she had approached him, at first tentative and scared, and how he had faced her with strength and determination in his eyes.

But then things started to go bad, even in that first week, and now, at the end of the second week, she had become so angry at him, at his insouciance, at his arrogance, at his bold determination to take advantage of her, that she had flown into a rage, and before she knew what was happening, she had found herself loading the gun, shaking with fear at the thought of killing another living thing.

What had started out as a perceived amity had turned to anger, resentment, misunderstanding, and most of all, revenge. He had taken advantage of her, violated her and the sanctity of her home. Something had overtaken her that final day of their relationship, and as she held the gun level with his chest, he had neither flinched nor made any effort to retreat. It was as if the whole thing had been predetermined, predestined, and she felt herself squeezing the trigger—the way her husband had demonstrated so many times at the firing range—feeling the power that she held in her hand, feeling the kickback, feeling the thrust of the metal object as the bullet sailed through the air and into his chest.

He had not fallen at first, but staggered, wild-eyed at her and then knelt on his knees, as if he were begging forgiveness for what he had done. But it was too late for that now. She had suffered too much in their short relationship and now she was ready to confess everything in the hope that her husband would support her.

Three days later, when her husband returned, she greeted him with her usual aplomb at the airport, trying to hide the truth of what had happened. Only small talk was passed between them as they rode through New York, over the George Washington Bridge, and into New Jersey.

When they pulled into the driveway, she stopped the car, turning the ignition off in such a way as to let him know that she had something to tell him. It was that little extra pause that occurred after turning the key—the way her hand lingered on it, then dropped to her side. She saw him wait, tired from his trip, but with the realization that something was coming. After a deep breath, she gripped the steering wheel and let it out:

"I shot a buck this week," she heard herself say, feeling as though the words had simply fallen out. She knew that it was illegal to kill the animal within the city limits and that she wasn't supposed to have gone near the gun. Her husband had warned her that it was off-limits; only to be used in case someone broke into their home. But in her mind, the deer *had* been an intruder.

"He totally destroyed my azaleas, most of the hostas, and every single geranium bloom. He only left the leaves on those," she said, looking her husband directly in the eye now, almost on the verge of tears. "I hated to do it, but I was so enraged," and with the last word her voice seemed to take on an unearthly quality, as if something from the depths, deep inside her had come forth, reborn after hundreds of years of waiting. She wasn't even conscious of her husband's hand as he reached out to comfort her, knowing how she loved and cared for animals, knowing how she would never hurt a living thing, remembering how she had forced him to find a way of ridding the garage of mice—of finding some way other than poison or death or violence. She hoped he knew what she must have gone through, not only because of her love for wildlife, but her fear of guns as well. But she was literally shaking.

"He was there every day," she said, her eyes wild and widening. "And he was so arrogant, as if he was testing me." She wasn't speaking to her husband now, but rather looking ahead, into space. "He was so beautiful, but so destructive. I had worked so hard on that garden," she continued, "and to have that animal ruin it day after day after day . . ." She trailed off, but her eyes still focused ahead, as if she had seen something she didn't know could exist, as if she had called up some part of her which she feared, yet was fascinated by.

"It was odd." she was saying, still not conscious of her husband's touch. "It was as if some long-lost part of me reached out and connected for a moment with the beast, and then something happened. I want to call it rage, but it was more than that. It was . . ." and here she paused and her eyes seemed to brighten and fill with terror simultaneously, "as if I was supposed to do it, as if hundreds of thousands of years of survival had come into play. It was . . ." and at this point she turned to her husband, in the hope of connecting with him for a moment, in the hope that he would share her anguish, her guilt, her camaraderie of killing simply because he was a man, "It was as if I had decided not to be the hunted, but rather the one who hunts."

They sat for quite some time, until the stillness of the evening came down upon them like a widow's veil—soft but without hesitation. She needed this time alone with him. She had experienced something terrible and strange and new and wonderful. She was confused and thought maybe he could help her understand. But she knew deep down that the power she had felt, the rage, the urge, the desire, the fear, would not go away, and that the act of killing another living thing, even if it had only been a deer, would forever be with her and color her being for the rest of her life, chasing her with thrill and guilt—running through the forest, a part of the hunt.

After a while, when the earth had cooled and the insects had begun their ritual songfest, she moved for the door handle of the car. It was dark as both of them left the vehicle—the doors making a pair of modern thuds—and continued into the suburban house. It would be some time the next day before either of them mentioned the incident again, and it would be another two days before she summoned the courage to show her husband where she had buried the body.

MORNING GLORY

The garden was alive with activity this early morning as Alma bent over a bed of newly planted impatiens, their jelly-bean colors spreading out like some child's imaginary banquet of sweets. Everywhere about her there was life—a blue jay wrestling with the remnants of a walnut shell; the neighbor's cat stealthily stalking some imagined garter snake or mouse; the scurrying of some unseen animal under a swath of ivy, fleeing the morning sun that had broken through canopies of hemlock that hovered too near the back of the house. The constant hum of the air-conditioner's backside sticking out from the house, along with its regular dripping into a fern (not her doing) that had recently sprung up to take advantage of the constant moisture, somehow soothed her. It was a reminder that if all else failed, she could always retreat to the cool kitchen for seclusion and comfort. For a brief moment this played in her mind, but there was too much to do and too little time—the cool interior of the house would have to wait. She was on a mission. Alma bent further over to study the flowers, feeling time at her back like some mean-spirited schoolyard bully intent on pushing her into the lake at a graduation picnic.

Her ample buttocks stretched the faded cotton blue-and-yellow floral-print pant material to capacity, the middle seams clinging to each other like survivors of a shipwreck attaching themselves to the last vestiges of a lifeboat. She was at a perfect ninety-degree angle now, surveying the damage that someone or something had done to the grouping of multi-colored flowers, their heads neatly snipped off. This would not do. Some action had to be taken. Finding a place in her mind to store this information, she moved on to a group of tiger lilies now biblically trumpeting their religious-tinged animal mouths toward the sky—orange horns of Gabriel; fierce jungle cats, yawning in the humid air. Christians and lions all in the same plant. At least these had remained unscathed. No need to stop here—there was work to be done. Her eyes moved on to a group of fairy roses whose long searching stems bent under the weight of their inexhaustible heads. Bright pinks and clean whites all jockeyed for position next to a now-too-spreading azalea.

Immediately the azalea brought back memories. She had planted it with her husband six years ago, before his sudden death. A heart attack had taken him in his sleep and she had lain all night, unknowingly, next to him. The doctor said that death had occurred sometime around nine o'clock, meaning that even as Alma had awakened at three in the morning for a glass of water, his demise had gone unnoticed. She shivered now at the thought of it, but at the time she had been too preoccupied with the shock of losing him for the fact to take hold. Some things took a while to sink in.

She knelt next to the flowering shrub now, eager to pull the weeds which were taking root in the delicate leaf-shaded area. She would dispose of them somewhere, where they could no longer multiply. Then she stopped. Something was wrong—that feeling again. That sensation of no sensation. Suddenly she couldn't remember why she was here or what she was supposed to do. She looked around the garden for an answer. Five spaced-apart fuzzy question marks confronted her and the present conundrum. It took a few minutes to realize that the punctuation marks were attached to squirrels. The small animals' inquisitive faces, their white underbellies, the small paws held together like polite church-going women holding muffs, pulled her mind from the anxiety of forgetting, and some inner wheel in her head snapped back into place. She was once again confronting the prolific weeds before her.

She felt a sense of unease. The forgetting had set that off. But no time to think about that now. There was ivy to be pulled from the rim of the goldfish pond—the one her son had built the year before he went away to war, never to return to the spindle bed of his youth, its earth-toned plaid bedspread never having been touched since. There was the barbecue grill now covered with poison ivy—many a family gathering had been put together over that. And there was the small statue of Cupid that she and her husband had bought on a trip—a gift to themselves for having stayed together fifty years. It now needed straightening since a large pine bough had skewed its presence, its arrow pointing directly toward the garbage cans near the kitchen door—a bad omen to Alma if ever there was one. There were roses to be pruned, aphids to be assaulted, and geraniums to be snipped. Everything about the garden was desperate.

Suddenly she stopped. Something was wrong. Yesterday there had been a blank piece of earth between the rock wall and a group of sedum. In the space was now a funnel of daises. They looked upward at her with plain, flat, matter-of-fact faces. She knelt beside them, noticing a white tag that was attached to one of the stems. Fingering it, she began to make out the name of her town's garden center. Then it came back to her: She had bought these late yesterday and planted them just before the sun had gone down. For a moment she let herself think. It was happening again, just as she had been told it would. Sinking down onto the cool, moist earth she allowed herself to inhale the smells of the garden: boxwood, leaf mold, the pungent and acidic smell of crushed geranium leaves.

She took off her tattered straw gardening hat and felt the rim. A good three inches was eaten away, the direct result of having left the article on the patio one night several months ago. Something had chewed off a good portion. It pained her that she was able to remember this and not the daises. It made no sense to her, this thing that was taking over her life, even though it had been explained to her at the doctor's office. No tests had proven anything certain, but his diagnosis had been devastating just the same—like hearing about a loved one's unexpected death. She had forced herself to visit the physician after discovering the telephone in the refrigerator, her eyeglasses on the top shelf in the hall closet, and a carton of milk under the sink.

"Alzheimer's," he had said to her, looking up over the top of his bifocals. "Nothing is certain, but all the signs point to it. Could be a slow process, or a more rapid one. We just have to wait and see."

So that was it. The thought of losing one of the last things she had left—her memories—was too much. With no husband and her child gone, the only thing for her was her garden. And now time was running out. There was so much work to be done. She had to leave something behind—something to show the world that she had been here—and yet the forces of nature seemed against her. She knew that someday the house would be sold, that she would be gone and forgotten, and she wanted the new owners to appreciate the work that had been put into this landscape. The flowers were her legacy, her only hope of not being forgotten, and now something had snipped off the heads of her impatiens, things were creeping up where they shouldn't, and the rhododendron hadn't even bloomed. But there wasn't time to waste on worrying about such matters. There was only the now, the present—slipping into the black hole of the past.

Quickly, while the pieces of her mind were in place, she tried to focus on the task at hand. There was no time to look for the garden spade. A bricklayer's trowel would have to do. She had no time to think about how the trowel had gotten here, lying next to the trellis. She only had time to act in the few given moments she might have left before the interruption came again. And again and again, each time taking more of her away.

She was now digging furiously at the base of the trellis, loosening weeds, aerating the earth, moving soil about, straightening the long stems of a morning glory vine that curled upward in the early sun. The nascent buds were just beginning to open, to show their colors that bled from the base of the flowers to their bell-shaped mouths. She knew she had to work fast, to fix things, to make something of her garden, to leave her mark, for in an hour or so the flowers would be in full bloom, extolling their glory for all to see, and by noon they would again be closed.

MY BROTHER NEAL IN PENSACOLA

Gertie had a firm grip on the azalea bush. She had managed to drag it the length of her block by the time she caught sight of her neighbor, Sue Rathway. The two women regarded each other as Gertie slouched up the driveway of Sue's home, or rather what had been her home. By now, the root-ball of the poor azalea shrub was worn almost completely down, but its vibrant fuchsia blooms still looked fresh as the first day of spring.

"Looks like that thing fared better in the storm than my house," said Sue, her hands firmly planted on her hips, her brow furrowed as she looked down at the flowering specimen.

Gertie regarded her small shrub as if it were some neighbor's child she had been asked to keep an eye on—one that she wasn't necessarily that emotionally attached to, but that needed looking after. "Was the only thing left that I could find," said Gertie, holding her other hand above her eyes and looking around to survey the damage. "Was the only thing the tornado didn't get," she said. "Funny how them tornados is." She waited, hand still shielding her eyes, still looking at Sue. Then she went on. "I'd heard stories about how them tornadoes'll take everything away, completely destroy a home, and leave a piece of paper untouched and in the exact place you left it. Can't figure how they do it, but they do. Pulled this bush clean out of the ground, but not a blossom touched. Must be the Lord's work."

"Well," answered Sue, "wasn't anything left untouched in my house, not even a piece of paper, much less a shrub. About the only thing that Harold could find (and at this point, both women turned their gaze to the well-muscled and tanned male who was digging through the rubble of his once-suburban-tract-home) was a used car seat we had when Ellen was eleven years old. And we don't need that any more, now that she's grown and away at college." Both women waited again, hoping something would change, hoping that they would wake up from the debacle they had just experienced. "You going to plant that thing again?" Sue finally asked.

"Lord, I don't know," answered Gertie. "Still, it's the only thing I've got left. I lost everything, just like most people did. The Bufords, they lost both those new cars and the patio furniture that Carol's mother-in-law give 'em, not to mention everything else. Most everybody's house is flat. Just flat."

"I think this was about the worst tornado I've seen," said Sue, motioning for Gertie to have a seat on what appeared to be a child's overturned and mangled playhouse. The miniature abode had blown in from two doors down. Gertie sat, still maintaining a firm grip around one of the azalea's branches. She gently fingered the trumpet-like blooms that shot out from the leathery green leaves.

"No," said Gertie in response to Sue's comment, "worst was back in 1974, leastwise that I could remember. That wasn't really one tornado, but a series of 'em. They say we had forty-seven in one day."

"I wasn't living here, back then," said Sue. "We hadn't moved from Utah yet and both my parents were still alive, so I know we weren't here at the time." There was a pause. "You think that one was worse?" she asked.

"Lordy, yes, yes, yes. That series that come through here just about took every man, woman, child, and tree out. At least this one left us debris. We still got pieces of cars and refrigerators. Back then there wasn't nothing left." Both women sat in silence for a moment and then Gertie added, "Still, it could be worse."

"How's that?" asked Sue as she surveyed a camper that had been cut completely in two, almost as if the deed had been done with a large electric carving knife used for a Thanksgiving turkey.

"Oh, you know. There's lots of things worse than having your house destroyed. Take my brother Neal in Pensacola. He's had it much worse than this," said Gertie, and pulled the azalea closer to her calves. "Why he had his whole life destroyed, and I don't mean by no tornado neither."

"Hurricane?" asked Sue, thinking about the damage the huge storms caused. She couldn't imagine living on the Gulf coast. No, southern Georgia was close enough to the coast for her.

"No. No hurricane. Something worse. Something that devastated his entire family." Gertie looked around the neighborhood, trying to decide whether or not to tell Sue the story. She casually waved a blow-fly away from her face.

"Well, what?" asked Sue, adjusting herself atop the brightly colored children's playhouse. Her legs kicked unknowingly at a green plastic chimney that was sticking out from the side.

"Well, I guess it's okay to tell. You're not anyone who's going to run into him anywhere, and besides, most of the family has moved on up into South Carolina, and well, Neal, well, we're not sure where he is . . ." Gertie trailed off. Sue waited, thinking that if she didn't prod any further, Gertie would offer up the devastation that had rained down on her brother Neal. Sure enough, it worked.

"Seems that Neal was out of work one summer back in '93. That was that summer we had the drought, remember? Anyway, he was at home and had just gotten a new table saw. Now, that in itself wasn't such a big deal, but rather, just a part of the problem. See, we thought we knew Neal, but I guess we didn't. No, thinking back on it now, none of us knew him."

"What do you mean? Why, what was there about him that you didn't know?" asked Sue.

"Well, for one, he was a cross-dresser. Now if that don't stop you in your tracks, I don't know what will."

"But how did you find out?"

"Well now, that's why I'm telling that you can be worse off than being hit by a tornado. That's what I'm tryin' to tell you. It wasn't that Neal just liked to cross-dress, but he was also into all them spa kind of treatments, you know?"

"Facials, tanning?"

"Yeah, right. That sort of thing. Especially the facials. I guess that was where it really started. He had evidently sent off for this new face mask from Miami. You know, one of those that you cake on and have to leave for half a day until it dries out? Well, one day while his wife was at work—like I said, he was out of a job that summer—he decides to give himself a facial. Idle hands. The work of the devil. Lord, I don't know how he gets himself into these messes, but he does. Why a groad man would want to play around with women's things is beyond me." Gertie took another swat at the blow-fly which wasn't taking the hint. Then she continued.

"Now, they only had one car between them and since his wife has to go to work, she takes it and leaves him at home to do whatever he does. So there's Neal, towel wrapped around his hair, all this green goo on his face, and relaxing in his wife's frilliest negligee." Gertie stopped again. She surveyed the damage done to a neighbor's birdbath, now sitting in what was left of a tree. Then she turned back to Sue who was anything but inattentive. "It was a special number that his wife had gotten at one of them chic garage sales near Atlanta and just never worn—silky, with those fake marabou feathers?" She waited, as if to give Sue time to appreciate the gown's design, a typical Southern question mark of inflection at the end of her sentence that, in any other part of the country, would have been a statement.

"Anyway. There was Neal, all made up with the negligee on. Now I told you he had just gotten a table saw. Neal might have been a cross-dresser out of a job, but he still liked to work with his hands and he made these Adirondack chairs for the neighbors from time to time. So, while he still has this facemask on, and while he's still wearing this fancy negligee, he decides to go out to the garage and fool with the saw. Let me tell you, my brother Neal is a lot of things, but bright is not one of them. Well, sir, the blade must not have been on tight, because just as soon as he starts up the motor, the thing flies off and cuts a huge gash in his arm, about the size of, oh, five or six inches long." Gertie made a gesture with her thumb and first finger over her arm to give an added visual effect. It worked, for Sue's lips curled slightly back. By this time, Sue's eyes were glued to Gertie who was too caught up in the story to notice her neighbor's expression.

"So naturally, he panics as any semi-sane person would do, and he runs in the house and calls an ambulance, totally forgetting that he's got this mud mask on and a marabou-trimmed nightgown. Did I mention he had matching slippers?"

"No, you forgot that part," said Sue, and squirmed on top of the now-defunct playhouse.

"Well, he did," said Gertie, rolling her eyes. "So he's in there, in the house, tying up a dishrag around his arm, trying to get the bleeding to stop, when he just up and passes out. We're not sure if it was the sight of blood or the lack of it, but there he was, on the kitchen floor, out cold, wearing a towel around his head, a mud mask, and his wife's clothing. Now, as if that weren't bad enough, they had this big old German shepherd named Bix who they had only had about a month. Neal's wife had picked the thing up at the pound because she insisted that she had heard a burglar trying to break in one night, and Neal had agreed to the dog because he was there all day and could use the company. But the pound had told them that the dog was neutered. The only problem was, he wasn't. And that thing was just as randy as they come."

"What would that have to . . ." Sue stared to ask, but one look at Gertie and she stopped.

"I'm getting to that," said Gertie holding up a flat hand, then folded her arms in front of her. "Now, all this didn't come together until later—until after the paramedics came and until after we pieced everything up—but I'll tell you so you can see why something like this is worse than any tornado."

"Okay, go on," said Sue.

"It seems that the dog was owned by a woman who was now serving twenty-five-to-life for several crimes, the least of which wasn't having sex with animals. She was this well-to-do high-society type up there close to Atlanta who had moved down here from Boston. Those Yankees. I'll tell you. Anyway, totally unknown to all of us at the time, Neal's wife had bought this marabou-trimmed nightgown from a garage sale up near Atlanta—the garage sale of the very woman who had been arrested for having sex with animals. So now you've got this dog *and* the nightgown that the woman used to own. Must have had her smell on it. That, and probably a few other things. I don't think I have to tell you that those two things, the dog and the negligee, would not make for a very good situation.

"Now here's the really weird part of the story," Gertie went on, "and this is just how my brother's luck tends to run. I mean, if there's anything that can go wrong, he'll step right in it." At this point Gertie stopped to regard a neighbor of Sue's across the street, pulling what was left of a bed frame across the driveway.

"I think I'm going to need a cigarette," said Sue, catching the opening in the conversation.

"Just wait. It gets worse," said Gertie and brushed her hair back. "What do you think the chances are that not only had Neal's wife bought the used negligee from that deranged woman, but that she somehow ended up with that woman's dog? You heard right. I'm telling you, Neal has all the wrong kind of luck. And this was the very dog that the woman had been *caught* with."

"I feel woozy," said Sue.

"You and me both. But just wait. So there's Neal, all laid out on the cold linoleum kitchen floor, with the towel on his head and the mud mask and the gown, and here comes Bix, all snorting and randy. Well, to make a long story short, when the paramedics arrived, there was Neal, out cold, being humped by this hundred-and-fifty-pound German shepherd and made-up to the hilt."

"What did they do?"

"They did what any God-fearin' paramedics would do—they took a picture. And that's not all. They had a video camera, so they took some film of the whole thing."

"Well, what happened after that?" asked Sue, at once both repelled and intrigued.

"Well, they took Neal to the hospital and got him all sewed up and put back together good as new, but when his wife came home, he had to tell her what had happened. He really didn't have a choice. Pensacola is not *that* big of a town and we were all surprised that nobody phoned her at work. Guess they felt sorry for her."

"How sad," said Sue and jumped down off the playhouse. "Did they get a divorce? What happened?"

"Divorce? There wasn't no time for a divorce. Neal's wife took what she could carry and left town that day. But I ain't done yet," she continued. "After his wife left and after that whole fiasco, he comes up and discovers that he's got the crabs."

Sue just looked puzzled.

"Crabs," Gertie repeated, leaning forward to give the word emphasis. "Body lice. Must have picked 'em up when the dog was tryin' to do his business."

"Oh," said Sue sheepishly.

"Yeah. Right. That's what I mean. And as if Neal hadn't learnt his lesson yet—the one that said he didn't have a brain in his head—he goes and decides to get some of that A-200 lice removal to get rid of the little varmints."

Sue just stared blankly.

"Honey, A-200's got kerosene in it and poor Neal's a chain smoker. He tried to light up after he dosed himself with that stuff and they say you could see the flames three blocks away. He just got out of the burn unit last week," said Gertie, and hopped down from her plastic perch. "So you can see where I'd think there are worse things than this here tornado. Either way, you can lose everything."

Sue nodded and for a time the two women didn't say anything. They just looked up at Sue's husband who was gingerly traversing the remnants of a roof beam.

Then Gertie spoke: "Well, it looks like I better be getting back. Sun's going down. I'm going to go talk to them Red Cross people they got set up over where the high school used to be. You going to be all right?"

"I'll be fine," said Sue and touched Gertie's arm. "You be careful getting back home now," and with that the two women turned from each other. Gertie walked back down the drive, still pulling the solitary azalea bush behind her. A few of the blooms had fallen off and the bush was beginning to show signs of wear.

Sue looked up at her husband—tall, sinewy, silhouetted in the dying sunlight. He appeared to be digging through some debris along about where the bathroom should have been. After a moment he stood up, turning over some object in his hand.

Sue waited.

"Harold?" she asked loudly, trying to get his attention, but her husband was deep in thought, lost in the contents of an unscathed jar of cold cream. She watched as he unscrewed the lid and dipped one of his fingers into it, gently rubbing it on his sunburned face.

"Harold!" she screamed, but Harold didn't hear her and in panic she began to pick her way through the debris toward him as he stood atop the pile of timbers that had once been their home.

"Harold, wait a minute . . . don't do that!" she called up to him, never stopping for a moment to inspect the remnants of her life that lay all about her. "Harold! Harold! . . ."

ROTHKO IN CONNECTICUT

Carol passed the time looking out the window of her study, waiting for her computer to reboot itself and come to life again. "How many Pulitzer Prize-winning moments have been lost waiting for these infernal machines to wake up?" she thought to herself as she scanned the large backyard surrounded by woods. Thickets of bare trees stretched for miles in back of the stream which ran behind the property. It was winter now and their brown watercolor-sketched outlines were dotted with occasional crows or squirrels. "Computers are supposed to be smart and quick," she said to herself. "That's why we gave up so much in the name of technology." She peered down at the impersonal cold metal box making grinding noises, then up again at the sky, clear and blue, framed by the trees. A snowstorm the day before had dumped more than twelve inches on the Connecticut town she lived in and everything had the look of a Currier and Ives lithograph. Even the ugly blue canvases covering woodpiles—their interiors home to a family of rats in the winter and garter snakes in the summer—were hidden. The effect was like Breughel's *Hunters in the Snow.* It seemed that everything in life reminded her of some work of art. Amazing what a few courses in college could do. She fondly remembered these classes and for good reason: It was where she had met her husband John.

They had both been freshmen at the time, taking an elective class in order to break the first-year monotony of required English and political science. It had been a slow romance at first—coffee and homework in the student union building; walks around campus between classes. It had so gradually progressed into an intimate relationship that neither had been aware of how deeply they had become involved. There was never any proposal of marriage with bended knee with dramatic setup. There were no announcements at family gatherings while someone called for everyone's attention. No, it had happened quite naturally and quietly. It had been assumed by both parties that they would get married just as both parents and relatives had also assumed it.

Now the love that she shared with her husband, John, had grown into something deeper, but deeper or not, she wished he were here to help her with her hard drive, instead of outside in the snow.

She looked down at the computer. It gurgled and hummed. The metal box containing every word she had ever written continued its internal mastications. She thought how funny this god in a box was. It seemed that everyone was worshiping these things. "And the geeks shall inherit the earth," she mused as she waited for her god to come to the rescue with bits of her life she had written down earlier that week. The short story she had promised the magazine was due in three days and she wasn't exactly sure what it was going to be about.

While she straightened out bits of her desk in an attempt to placate her frustrations with technology's latest upgrade on speed and globalization, she simultaneously pondered the miracle of science and technology. Man was on the verge of producing computer chip implants that would enable the blind to see and those who had been previously paralyzed to move inanimate limbs. By the time she had completed the thought the scientists and computer moguls had probably completed that task and were moving on to greater achievements. "The lame shall walk and the blind shall see," thought Carol as she gently nudged the computer monitor, then gave it a good whack. She was from the old school of thinking about machines which said that if you kicked the thing hard enough (think Coke machines in the fifth grade which had eaten your last quarter), some emotional mechanism would respond within all the gear and wheels, and feeling guilty, the boxed metal monsters would produce the desired Nehi or grape soda, or worst case scenario, relinquish their hold on a portion of that week's allowance.

The noises didn't sound healthy to her, but she had been told by friends who made their living observing, fixing, and excusing such things, that everything was under control. Soon one of the many messages came to the screen asking her for some bit of information. While it was almost always an issue not terribly important, she still agonized over her choice to continue by clicking "yes." It had always amazed her how, when seeking the help of a friend or her husband, they would stand over her so coolly, choosing "yes," or "continue" to questions asked about virus checks or saving to disks. She would have been angst-ridden for hours about what the result might have been, when they simply chose and continued, usually so fast that she didn't have a chance to view the message or question.

It seemed to be the same with her life. She could agonize over the smallest detail and yet John, her husband, effortlessly made decisions, the results of which never seemed to be wrong. "Perhaps this is the reason for my anxiety today." She said this to herself as she watched John from the second-story window of their Westport, Connecticut, home. He was by the stream which ran through the back of their property, boot-clad, and in heavy parka the same shade of green—dark, brooding, clever—as that of their den walls. His hand occasionally reached into some unseen area and then flung itself out as if sowing seeds in the spring. She marveled to herself how at this distance no sign of his Parkinson's disease was visible as he fed his beloved ducks and squirrels which gathered around him. Each month he spent over a hundred dollars on duck feed. That was another of the things that had first attracted her to him—his benevolence toward animals. It had a calming effect on Carol. Even his Parkinson's gave her something to focus on. She doted on him because of it, and while sad, she felt that she had secretly been given some great gift by being able to care for him.

"Windows has performed an illegal function. The system will automatically shut down. Do you want to save to a disk before exiting?" the screen in front of her questioned.

She shut the system down and waited the proverbial three seconds before rebooting. As much as she prided herself on being a Luddite, she couldn't bring herself to write in longhand. It was too much like something one of those authors professed to that you saw on television. Probably they all used a computer, but none would admit it. She was always amazed at how many non-sweater-wearing, accountant-looking authors spoke of actually *writing* out their words. Her hand cramped just thinking about it.

Besides, with all the revisions her editor wanted her to make, it wasn't practical to have your work in some format that couldn't be easily changed.

As she started the system again and waited, a genuine sadness came over her. Not because of her husband's recent downturn of health, but rather for the fact that it was finally beginning to sink in that they were going to have to sell the house. She realized that this view from her study—this view of the stream, the ducks, John slowly meandering about the winter-scape—would be gone for her someday. The house had been on the market now for some six months with no offers and this was causing her a mixture of emotions. The joy she was experiencing at prolonging her residence in the same house she had lived in for the past four years was mixed with the guilt of not having prodded the real estate agent more to show it.

The house would have to go soon, but deep down she wasn't in any hurry. She remembered what an experience it had been looking for a new place to live. She was at odds trying to decide which was worse: looking for a job, looking for a mate, or looking for a dwelling. She let out an unrestrained yawn and pulled the lint from her sweater. Her legs stretched out before her like two planks holding her in the chair. She felt at least some sense of relief that she didn't have to put too much energy toward this just yet—this house hunting. Their funds would hold out for a little longer. At least the stock market was momentarily good, and she felt certain that she and John would be able to glean a healthy profit from the sale of the house because of the extensive remodeling they had done.

They had decided to move to the town of Westport a little over four years ago. Their New York apartment had become smaller and smaller with each flea market purchase and added bookshelf until finally, on a dare from friends (that and the fact that New York real estate agents seemed to have a knack for ignoring the phrase "I only want to look at . . ." and anything that came after it), they had taken the train to Westchester one crisp fall day to look at two houses John had seen in one of the pamphlets he had found just inside the door of a SoHo supermarket.

As he had stood there in the vestibule of the Manhattan market, being jostled by elbows, brown recyclable bags, and shafts of fennel, he became immersed in the flat black-and-white photographs that represented far-off Cape Cods and colonials. How exotic they seemed to New Yorkers who had lived most of their lives in the city. In short, he had fallen in love with the idea of living outside Manhattan, or at least of having a small area of grass and trees that you didn't have to share with boom boxes and loud twenty-something people who played Frisbee and drank beer from paper-bag covered cans. You could have your own area where you didn't have to worry about being run over by a bicycle or having someone's loose dog walk over your stomach as you sunbathed in the Sheep Meadow in Central Park.

John and Carol perused the pamphlets together. Grainy black-and-white photos had stared out at them from the pages of the brochure: stately Tudors with sloping lawns and quaint chimney pots hovering high above the stucco-and-beam walls; bright Greek revivals with century-old rhododendrons; spare colonials all looking the same (not too much shrubbery, coach lanterns at the entrance, and a well-camouflaged garage). They had settled on the Tudor and the Greek revival on what was to be their only trip to Westchester, and made the arduous journey by train one cool Saturday. They had expected the cars of the train to be empty—this not being a work day—but they found instead noisy, rude passengers—different than the usually respectable group who frequented the line. An overweight and scantily clad black woman stuffed her face with popcorn while managing to talk non-stop on her cell phone. Two blond, overtly teenage girls giggled the entire way, occasionally holding up a foldout of a naked man from a women's magazine for the other passengers to see. A rather unctuous and portly man took up two seats and snored from Grand Central Terminal all the way to Tuckahoe.

When they arrived at the station of the town in which the Tudor was located, a lovely woman greeted them with the usual smile and brochures (tight linen suit, glasses on chain, a too-small handbag with a slight tear on the corner) and ushered them into her small foreign-made car. It smelled of old papers and leftover

McDonald's wrappers. They would see the Tudor first. As they turned down the street which Carol had been told the house was on, her heart sank. This wasn't a neighborhood for stately residences. The house in the picture was enormous, seemingly two blocks long with a yard big enough to put a swimming pool and tennis court in if in fact they didn't already exist.

Then she saw it, but her mind wasn't letting her believe what was in front of her. It was the same house all right, but some very creative photographer had managed to capture its best angle, and with the proper lens had conveyed the impression that the house was seven or eight times larger than it really was. This thing could have been the reproduction dollhouse for the one in the picture. And the entire yard was not much bigger than the size of her cubicle at work, and in Manhattan that meant small.

She looked over at John who was obviously disappointed but not showing his reaction to the guide. "They want $424,000 for this?" was all she could think of as they approached the front door which had looked so stately in the photo. It was a mere three inches taller than Carol, and John had to bend down to enter. While the outside was bad, with its miniature chimneys and casement windows just big enough for one arm to stretch through ("Aren't they lovely—and the whole effect is so English!"), the inside was even worse. The entrance hall floor was covered in mint-green bathroom tiles, and the walls, paneled in knotty pine, had been painted a dreary gray color. The large dark knots surfaced through the paint like teenage pockmarks through cheap makeup.

The living room was carpeted in sculpted green shag pile with one end of the room being a good three inches lower than the other as the house had sunk somewhat in a past rainstorm. Off to the side of the living room was the sun porch, now completely enclosed and dark. It smelled of urine and mothballs. Against its far wall stood an industrial-grade hospital bed, its occupant long ago deceased. Yellowed I.V. tubes were carelessly strewn atop the wrinkled, stained sheets that covered the obese and lumpy mattress.

Carol had tried to get the guide's attention, but the woman proceeded full steam up the filthy shag carpeting on the stairs. "It's good that the walls of the staircase are stucco," thought Carol, "because these steps are so narrow that I can barely manage. At least there's something to hold on to." She gripped the all-too-obvious trowel marks which swirled up and down the walls. By the time all three had reached the top of the stairs and turned to the first bedroom, the matron of the house, who had been noisily chatting on the phone during their entrance, had managed to pry herself from the receiver. She was now looking for them. While Carol was sure they had taken the owner by surprise, she nevertheless felt that once the doorbell rang it should have been perfectly acceptable for the woman to remove the cotton balls from between her toes and extinguish the extra-long menthol cigarette she was smoking. Evidently the woman of the house was not of the same opinion.

The owner was now beside them. She took a long drag on the cigarette, her aging crepe-textured lips closing in tightly around the filter. Exhaling, she started in. "This bedroom was all custom designed," she rang out, completely taking over the real estate agent's duties. The agent cowered near a pile of dirty polyester clothes in the corner, which filled what looked like a baby's crib. "You can see the lovely woodwork. I had a designer come in and do the whole thing, and . . . STEVEN! . . . STEVEN!" she now yelled in the direction of the stairs, "WHAT DID WE PAY TO HAVE THIS WOODWORK DONE?" She waited, her left hand supporting her right elbow, the cigarette hovering slightly to the right of her face. The smoke curled lazily around her and looked for the nearest exit as if repelled.

"STEVEN?" she yelled again in the direction of the stairs, and then proceeded to chew on one of her fingernails. She extracted a sliver of nail and spat it out on the pink carpeting. "STEVEN . . . WHAT DID . . ." she went on yelling, but was interrupted from below.

"I DON'T KNOW WHAT WE PAID. I'LL TRY TO FIND A RECEIPT!" a slovenly-voiced young man answered, his decibel volume matching hers.

"It's not really that important," said the real estate agent, her normal voice contrasting with that belonging to the lady of the house and this invisible person named 'Steven.' "I'm sure we can . . ."

"WELL WHAT DO YOU THINK WE PAID FOR IT? STEVEN? STEVEN?" An uncomfortable pause. "STEVEN?" She clicked one chipped nail against the other. The sound reminded Carol of the left-turn signal on her last car before she totaled it.

Carol tried to change the subject. "What a lovely bedspread," she said, completely lying through her teeth. It was an insipid, faux-satin pink number with so many stains on it that it looked like a bad Jackson Pollack imitation concocted out of Pepto-Bismol.

"Oh, that," said the lady of the house, speaking now in normal tones, "I had my designer make that to match the lamp shades," and she gestured toward two dime store lamps sporting pink lace shades. One was cocked at a forty-five degree angle and torn in three places. The matron fingered it roughly, trying to get the thing to sit up straight, her long hands shaping it as if it were a wig on a head-stand, her index finger making sure the cigarette never touched the fabric. "Francis chewed this up last week because we had her fixed. You know how snippy poodles can be," she said as she gave up and then walked into the next room.

Carol had thought that was the cue to follow the woman, and she and all the others had shuffled after her, but when they entered the next bedroom, the woman was gone, having exited through another door, and the real estate agent was left to conclude the tour. They all looked at one another as if one of them had the explanation for the woman's sudden disappearance. Somewhere on the top floor, a toilet whined, perpetually losing water, and a bathroom sink dripped spasmodically in the distance. An enormous shudder from the pipes in the walls sounding somewhat like two barges colliding convinced Carol that it was time to leave.

So that day Carol and John had decided to give up on Westchester. They hadn't even bothered to look at the Greek revival, imagining it to be on the same level as the Tudor, if not worse. Weren't Greek revivals supposed to be in Georgia, anyway?

When they saw their present Connecticut house for the first time they had again been less than thrilled. John had motioned to the real estate agent (this time a man—thick-set, dark glasses, light blue socks and black pants) trying to get his attention before he even put the key in the door. This was not a house either of them wanted. The agent had barreled through the front door, and as John was in the process of signaling him again, both he and Carol had stopped. John had turned to the agent, and by judging the look in Carol's eye had said simply, "We'll take it." The outside wasn't much to look at, but the inside was magnificent.

When the agent managed to pick his lower jaw up from the floor, he ushered them back to the office, a few miles down the road. His age-spotted hands shook as he filled out the necessary paperwork. Carol and John smiled at each other: Their first home together. There was no getting past the charming wallpaper, the heavy crown moldings, the French doors which opened onto the sunroom.

The last few years in the house had been bliss. Of course there had been minor problems at first. Not with the house—with the neighborhood or rather the neighbors. John had shown more than a reasonable dislike at first for the two gay men who lived diagonally across from them. Their backyard overlooked that of the two men, and while it was immaculate year-round, John didn't like having to view the lawn of, as he termed it, "Some deviate couple." Carol had long been used to the company of gay men, having worked with them at her job in the city.

She remembered her first encounter with the gay world. It was at a party given by fellow dancers of her modern dance class at New York University. Each Tuesday and Thursday for a year before the party, she and the others would make their way to the Village loft to stretch and moan, their torn leotards and shabby leg warmers displayed like proud battle scars. She somehow found the smell of damp clothes, sweat, and the sound of the badly out-of-tune piano to be life itself as the class followed the eagle-eyed instructor. One day toward the end of the year, a lithe young man had handed her an invitation to a loft in SoHo. She had gone, eagerly anticipating her first New York party alone as John was working late. The celebration was only blocks from their SoHo loft.

At the gathering she had made the acquaintance of one of the new dancers in the class, someone who had come in late, mid-semester. His name was Cary. He was long and lean with an angelic face and a head of curly brown hair falling damply over his chestnut eyes. She had fallen in love with him—not literally as she was already married to John—as she found in him all the qualities she thought a man should own. All except one. Cary could talk about music and art for hours, he was muscular and had a pleasant smile and handshake, and he kept himself in shape both mentally and physically as if waiting for his perfect princess to emerge from the shadows and take his hand. Carol had imagined his girlfriend—equally tall, maybe a successful woman who owned her own catering business. She would have soft brown hair. They would name their first child Jason, and Cary would eventually become danseur premier in the New York City Ballet. Her idealization had been dashed at the party when Cary's boyfriend met him near the oversized Ikea bowl containing cheese puffs and party mix, and gave the dancer a warm hug and a kiss on the lips.

She marveled at her ignorance at the time, both before she knew of Cary's sexual orientation, and afterward. She had imagined, even after she had visual and intellectual proof of his gayness, that he was different from the others. All gay men weren't like Cary. They couldn't be, or else the women of the world were really missing out on something. Weren't gay men effeminate, overly slim, affected, and somewhat nerdy? Then slowly she encountered others. There was Jim, the handsome young man who worked at the health food store she frequented. He was rugged and quiet, but he was not above making eyes at the Puerto Rican stock clerk, and he occasionally made advances toward the boy when he thought no one was looking. There was Alfredo, who sold the Bolivian sweaters and handmade leather purses at the street fairs. He was always giving her a good price and eager to talk about what men really want, frank about his sexuality, assuming that everyone would accept him with his Latin swagger and smoothness.

She had found the whole experience educational. Still, there was a point she reached when she felt a tired disappointment, a disillusionment of sorts, and a feeling that there was more sameness in the world than difference. It was the same feeling you had when, seeing an artist's work displayed among others in a gallery, you marveled at his technique, his originality, his soul on exhibit for all to see. You marveled at his ability to create one singular work which could never be repeated. You imagined him secluded in his studio, inclement weather outside, with only a small fire in the wood stove to warm himself. When he had put the last brush stroke on the canvas, you imagined him falling to the floor, looking upward toward the clanking water pipes to thank God for allowing him to express his innermost depths just this once on canvas with the aid of only a few badly squeezed tubes of paint. So intrigued with his work were you that you spent months waiting for his show to open. When the day arrived you lifted yourself up the metal stairs and into the gallery, ready to be swept into another dimension, only to be disillusioned. Each picture in the exhibit was almost exactly the same. Oh, there were subtle differences. One had a little more blue. One was slightly darker than the other. One was elongated, fresher, more alive. But they were, deep down, all the same picture. It was all variations on a theme.

Carol had experienced that with her first Rothko. She had been astounded to find a painting so original, so vibrant and brave, that later, when she found out that there were rooms full of them, all variations, she was less enamored. Then someone had pointed out to her that the vibrant colors had slowly grown darker with each painting the artist had produced, until he committed suicide. It had all made sense to Carol at that point. It wasn't that he had repeated himself, but rather that each painting meant something in relation to the one which had come before it. She began to see his work as a whole. A work in progress, only on a multitude of canvases.

The disturbing symbolism gripped at her as she thought of this. Maybe she had made the connection subconsciously, maybe not. She thought of gay men slowly becoming extinguished because of AIDS. They were like God's Rothkos—vibrant, young, alive, and healthy men in oranges and yellows, gradually turning to grays and browns, finally darkening until they disappeared. She wondered what kind of God would do that. She had always imagined God as an impressionist, but on further reflection, she thought it appropriate that he had a good deal of abstractionist in him. After all, who understood the universe, literally *or* art-wise? Then the thought: That we were all Rothkos. That we're all getting darker until we self-extinguished, maybe not from a disease, but just from living. Gay men seemed to have just speeded up the process—to be a smaller representation of the whole. Many of them seemed to live their lives in the fast lane, not necessarily with drugs or sex, but with *something*, as if they had been cheated out of their formative years by being different and now had to make up for lost time.

Yes, they were all different people, but it seemed to her that some genetic underhandedness was at play, giving them all somewhat similar qualities. Or maybe she only noticed the qualities because they were singled out as a group. Perhaps we all had these qualities. Still, she couldn't help but imagine that all gay men gasped at age five when they saw their first pink plastic flamingo, or squealed with delight at their first viewing of Marilyn Monroe's slinky leg kicking the lever in *Bus Stop*, lighting up the stage when she sang the words "I'm a flame." It had to be so, didn't it?

Carol wasn't sure anymore. She wasn't sure about anything. Maybe it was all her puerile attempts to make things fit into categories in the hope that life would follow her lead.

So Carol wrestled with giving up her preconceived notions, and now she made attempts at getting other people to do the same. Carol tried to reason with John about the neighbor's sexual orientation, but he would have none of it.

The two gay men had been welcoming individuals, bringing a cake over the first week of their arrival, letting Carol and John know that they were glad to have them in the neighborhood. Both men were from the South, and Carol had been enamored of their accents, gentleness, and the fact that they were both sturdily built and rugged looking. John's anti-gay attitude had softened later when he discovered the two men had a fully equipped tool shop, complete with several hard-to-find routers that the nearest Home Depot didn't carry. Gradually their evenness broke down John's defiant moods, and the three, John, Milton, and John (there were two on the block now) were always trading sanding belts or bits of useful information on mulch piles or the removal of poison ivy. So close had they become that Carol was always having to refer to one as "Gay John," and one as "My John." And because of their similarities and shared interests with Her John, she had had to once again reshuffle the deck of reasoning that had stereotyped the two men and their tribe.

Carol thought about them, her neighbors, as she looked out her window. John (Her John) had made his way over to the two men and was now locked in conversation with the other John, probably about something mundane and suburban like drill bits or window glazing. The two gay men had built four snowmen in the winter yard, and Her John was now admiring the handiwork between snippets of tool shop jargon.

The first grouping of snow people was of a man and woman, the man complete with top hat, and the woman in a snow rendition of a hoop skirt complete with sixteen-inch waist and puffed sleeves. It wasn't hard for Carol to figure out that the couple were supposed to be Rhett and Scarlet. If they could have made Hattie McDaniel and remained politically correct, they probably would have. "But what would you do," thought Carol, "put black face on a snowman?"

All the same, Southern roots ran deep and John and Milton were constantly displaying their "below the Mason-Dixon line" upbringing by either making some sort of overly sweet pastry which was distributed for welcoming newcomers, funerals, or birthdays, or by having one of their Southern food parties. Carol and Her John had been privileged to partake of these events from time to time and inevitably she came home across their insect-humming yard in the summertime with a plate of cornbread, collard greens, and smoked ham. She had fond memories of gingerly navigating through the overgrown azalea bushes Milton had planted years before while balancing a pie plate full of tomorrow's lunch, her hands shaking from too much to drink and her feet unsure on the slippery wet grass.

So it was only fitting that they had created a *Gone With the Wind* tableau in their Connecticut backyard. Rhett's surly looks stared back at her, his long stick arm firmly around Scarlet's waist. Scarlet had a demure but sly look, her appearance giving the impression that she was constantly on the lookout for her next husband. Most people would have built a snowman, stuck a carrot in the face, put two lumps of coal in for eyes, and called it a day. Not the two men who lived next door. They had somehow managed to give the two mounds of snow emotional histories and feelings. What a shame that these people made of something so fragile as frozen water crystals wouldn't last past the spring.

The other grouping of snow people, the ones a few feet away, were obviously two snowmen. Two *men.* No women allowed here. The good news was that Carol at least credited her neighbors with sticking the carrot in the proper place and not in some off-color location. After all, there were children about the neighborhood. The two snow-gents leaned slightly toward each other, their twig arms carefully entwined. Her John was now inspecting the two gay men's work, offering up a handful of cracked corn for non-existent mouths. The usual charcoal briquettes (fast-burning, no lighter fluid necessary) had been used for the eyes and two rather motley carrots stuck out for noses. Both gentlemen snowmen wore baseball caps (Yankees and Mets) and had a content look on their faces. Carol imagined post-coitus snow sex. She lingered over this thought for only a moment, then turned her attention back to the day inside where it was warm.

She shut off her computer, resolute in the fact that today's writing wasn't going to happen. Besides, she was thinking about Her John now, about his illness and how they were going to deal with it in the coming months. She was thankful for neighbors like Milton and Gay John, and selfishly she mused that it was good that the two men didn't have any children, that they were without all the trappings of heterosexuality. While she didn't want to think she would take advantage of them, she was glad they might have the moments to spare if Her John's illness got worse. Gay or not, they were two men and she might soon be a single and frightened woman, alone in the suburbs. They were her two Rothkos—not exactly the same, not exactly different. They were vibrant and beautiful in their own way. Maybe it was she who was the painting, getting darker.

It was getting late. She had sat for such a long time that her legs had fallen asleep. The sun was getting lower in the sky, illuminating the snow people Milton and Gay John had created. She saw her neighbors wave to Her John as he slowly and somewhat painfully made his way up the hill toward home—the house they would be selling soon, if they could find a buyer.

She watched his every move. An ordinary person wouldn't have noticed that there was anything wrong with him, but she knew. She remembered when the pain and tremors started, long before the endless waits in sterile, Muzak-filled waiting rooms. Long before she stopped, half-hoping to hear some good news when the doctor and Her John emerged from a battery of tests. He was getting closer now, carefully putting one foot in front of the other. Soon he would be nearing the rock garden, its sparse foliage completely dormant and awaiting the summer sun's excessive rays. Soon he would be making his way up the stone path, the one that Milton and Gay John helped to build last year as a birthday gift. Soon he would be entering the basement door, slipping out of his wet boots. He would slowly make his way upstairs.

He would pad up to the second floor. Carol could feel him getting nearer. She knew he would be asking about what, if anything, she had written. She would have to tell him that today was a bust, but not to worry—that she had an idea for a new piece. She would mumble something about writing of snow and friendship, of writing about loss, and art.

Soon his hand would touch her shoulder. They would stay like that for some time—him behind her, quiet, not saying a word as they both looked out at the silhouetted trees, the snow-covered garden, the snow people. In a few weeks the white blanket would melt, but the snowmen with their solidly packed torsos would remain for much longer. Carol knew that it would take most of the winter for them to disappear completely, even with a heavy rain. She knew it would be a while before they became just another memory, and she smiled as she reached up, thinking about how important this loaned time was to her, and took hold of his Her John's hand.

EARLY SUNDAY MORNING

Manly sucked in his breath as he pulled the vanity chair from his parents' bedroom and maneuvered it across the tiled bathroom floor. The chair's four metal feet clattered noisily over the small white octagon-shaped tiles which spread out like a vast ceramic plateau around the bathtub, sink, and commode. He was still wearing his pajamas—it was only nine-thirty on this Sunday morning—and as his mother and father were somewhere in the other end of their suburban house, reading the Sunday paper and drinking tepid coffee, he hoped they wouldn't hear him and thwart his intentions as they usually did.

It had happened again: The dream. He had become aware of the sun's dim rays filtering through the curtains this Sunday morning to find the same dream had manifested itself inside his head just a few moments before awakening. It had haunted him for some time, and it was always exactly the same.

He was in the living room, safely nestled on the fibrous silver-green area rug which covered the hard parquet-wood floor. It was night and the only sounds were those of a few cars passing by on the street. Somehow, in the dream as in real life, he found the sound of the vehicles comforting. They represented the fact that he was not alone in the world. Then, in the dream his father came into the room and picked him up. It happened each time, exactly the same way. They would waltz to the same record—he was only three years old in the nocturnal visitation—and his father could easily swing him around to the music. He always enjoyed the feeling of being held while the inertia of being flung around pulled him out into the room. They would both laugh, but something always went wrong. What it was he couldn't remember. Each time there was the music, the waltzing, the feeling of being floated around the room and then a blank. It was as if his mind was not letting him acknowledge what the blank was. Then he would begin to experience the second half of the dream, or at least the portion after the blank space. It too was always the same. It seemed that before he could enjoy the feeling there had been in the first half, the terror began—a racehorse anxious to get out of the gate. Suddenly the carpet became a flat silky pool of water, infinitely deep and dangerous as it turned itself into a vehicle of death. He was at the very center as it became a violent whirlpool, round and ominous like the blade of one of his father's circular saws in the tool shed.

His father was standing on the edge of the whirlpool with his back to him. No amount of crying could reach the man, and his father seemed to be unaware of the rope that extended itself from around his waist to Manly's grasping hands at the vortex of the swirling water. He always noticed the rope—its thick, fibrous, oily feel, as if it had just been pulled from a gigantic steamship and was here for his survival. He hated the touch of it, but he knew that if he wanted to survive, he would have to hold on to it. Each time he held on, he was overcome with a sick feeling, but hold on he did, for to him anything was better than being pulled into the whirlpool. Death by water.

How the dream ended, he couldn't say, and this, along with the bizarre subject matter—whirlpools, ropes, waltzes—always confused him when awakening. He could remember the beginning, then a blank. Then the second part and another blank. While the dream itself was terrifying, the blanks were even more so. He would wake with a metallic taste in his mouth and a sluggish feeling. Then there was the nausea he felt. He was feeling it now—it came and went—waves lapping at a shoreline in slow motion—and he feared it as if it were as powerful and unrelenting as the ocean itself. Underneath was that watery fear. The dream always had to do with water. The fear of drowning.

These dreams always seemed to happen for the most part on Saturday nights. He noticed which evening they occurred because his father was always getting drunk that night, coming home late, usually waking up at least some portion of the household. Then there was Sunday morning, when everyone seemed to recuperate.

Sundays were always the same for him. He had his own rituals to perform and today would be no different from the other Sundays. Only now he had to be more careful. His parents had caught on, and so now he used extra caution.

He thought about this as he climbed onto the light metal chair in order to reach the medicine cabinet in his parents' bathroom. This medicine cabinet had long played a part in his morning rituals and he hoped this morning would be no different. As he gripped the heavy mirrored door, he knew that his timing and balance in the handling of this first obstacle was most important. There are sounds within a household which everyone knows whether they are awake or asleep, and certain ones, because of past experiences, can set off a type of burglar alarm. He knew that the high-pitched squeak of the cabinet door as it made its way along the cold metal rod which connected it to the frame of the cabinet would be one of these noises. And he knew that the minute his parents heard it they would come—feet heavy-hitting the floor, pajamas flying loosely around them—straight to its source.

As carefully and slowly as he could, he pulled open the door, making sure to hold it with both hands so that he had control over the opening *snap* and subsequent low squeal of its connecting mechanism. All done with this portion of the task, he experienced the type of relief one feels after catching a glass in mid-air, having dropped it accidentally. He practiced calm as he took in the contents of the cabinet, having safely negotiated the precarious landscape that was secrecy.

The usual items were at hand: Barbasol shaving cream, the evaporating remnants of mad-dog foam curled up around its spout; a styptic pencil, its soft, porous white cylinder a stick of red-stripe-free peppermint; a brush with multi-colored strands of hair nestled within the forest of badger bristles; a comb with dandruff flakes imbedded every few teeth; a tube of toothpaste, its hourglass shape reeking of mint and antiseptic, witness to countless arguments between his parents over its form. Finally there was the coveted razor. But on closer inspection he realized the blade was missing. He searched around the different levels of the cabinet, thinking that perhaps there were some blades, but all that remained was the soap scum-laden metallic shaft and an empty and rather harmless place where the coveted blade should be.

He felt a wave of nausea as he picked up the comb and thought for a moment about what he would do next, taking in the contents which made their home within the enameled beige interior of the medicine cabinet. He ran his finger over the teeth of the comb. The flakes of dandruff floated onto the sink basin and the teeth produced a reverberation like that of a miniature xylophone belonging to a doll. The pitches pealed off the plastic instrument, disappearing upward into nothingness. He gently sat it back on the shelf in the exact position it had come from.

Then he spied it—one of the culprits which caused him so much anxiety. It was a small opening, about an inch long and exceedingly thin, on the back of the medicine cabinet wall. This was the opening that his father used to deposit his worn-out razor blades. There must be hundreds of them in there. If only he could get to them. And who had thought up this idea anyway—of putting used razor blades into a wall? Sure, he knew that you were supposed to dispose of blades properly so that no one got hurt, but who thought of dropping them down behind the wall of a bathroom? Was there some sort of box behind there that held them or did they just fall behind the bricks, the sheet rock, the plaster? What happened when someone tore down a house? Did the demolition men find thousands of razor blades (and anything else that would fit through the small opening) when the dust cleared? He imagined the workmen, dirt-covered and sweaty, with hands on hips, shaking their heads as a mountain of blades came tumbling out from the bottom of a wall recently dismembered by a huge wrecking ball. He couldn't hear what they were saying because of the rumble of bulldozers and jackhammers, but he imagined them pointing to the pile of dangerous little metal objects, not realizing that they were creating the same problem in the very homes they lived in with their own morning ablutions.

After a while Manly gave up on his quest for the blades, and shutting the cabinet as gently as he had opened it (the authoritative snap could just as easily send his parents running), he softly climbed down from the vanity chair and pulled it, this time less noisily, back into the bedroom.

He decided that the next place he would search would be his father's chest of drawers. It was, after all, the one place he had been forbidden to see the inside of. He couldn't say why the quest took this form—always wanting to use his father's things—but he knew that he never bothered to search through the hair nets, the rouge pots, the drawers of lipsticks and tweezers that made up the foreign landscape of his mother's world. For some reason it had to be his father's belongings. There was some unwritten law in the back of his mind that said so. So today it would be the chest of drawers that would be searched.

He imagined money, gold, incriminating pictures, and just about anything else valuable inside. Needless to say he was sorely disappointed when, after climbing up on the very same vanity chair (it was now positioned on the sculptured-pile carpeting which absorbed noises more readily), he slid open a drawer and looked inside. Socks married up perfectly, their black ribbing causing them to cling to each other like drunken friends on some bad sitcom he'd seen. Handkerchiefs all white, limp, with tattered edges nestled in one corner. A small shallow dish containing three dollars and fifteen cents in assorted change (he took the time to count it) crouched to one side. This was no treasure find. This was the ultimate in mundane.

Now his eye caught something. Some sort of small plastic squares within which was some other sort of plastic. Trojans? What was that? Why did something that appeared to have such an ephemeral life have such an ominous, heavy, authoritative name? His eyes continued to move about the drawer, locating next a velvet box, its black outer covering showing more than the usual collection of lint. The hinge squeaked as he opened it. Nothing here of interest—just two gold cufflinks in the image of Indian head pennies. He had never seen his father wear these. The man didn't wear French cuffs. These had been a gift from his mother to his father several years ago, and like so many gifts one gives to spouses and relations, they ended up being relegated to the back of sock drawers at best, if not in the garbage. Evidently these had some value, but he wasn't looking for cufflinks today. They wouldn't serve his purpose. He let the box close with its predetermined muffled snap and continued his search.

Just as he was feeling despondent, his eye caught something: a pack of cigarettes along with a small book of matches. He picked them up in his hand, the cellophane crinkling as he did so, and fingered the loose foil flap which protected the contents within. A good seven or eight cigarettes were contained inside the flimsy paper housing. They leaned against each other with a nonchalance reserved for intimate companions, and indeed, he imagined them quite friendly, having been cooped up in this pack, in this drawer, among these belongings for such a long time. He rarely saw his father smoke, and this surprised him, for he knew the man maintained several habits constantly, if not obsessively, and it struck him as odd that this habit, this semi-socially acceptable one, wouldn't be engaged in as often as some of the other nefarious ones he suspected or witnessed.

He felt a slight tinge of sadness as he removed one of the crisp white cylinders—as though he were God removing a friend from a tight circle of jocular teenagers in order to teach them a lesson; to teach them about the meaning of life through death. But the feeling was short-lived as he carefully placed the tobacco shaft into his pajama pocket along with the book of matches, and climbed down from the chair.

There was the sense of modified elation that one feels after winning a prize, though not fairly, or that one experiences after passing some test of strength or intellect, or both—if not by one's own wits, then by cheating. And it was probably this sense of tailored elation that carried him so uncaringly through the house, without fear of discovery, for as he made his way out a side door of the home and into the cool green morning of the backyard, he wasn't aware whether or not his parents had noticed his departure. It was only as he approached the tool shed that he became aware they were still engulfed in the morning paper and coffee. He could see them easily now through the sparse yew hedges which separated the shed from the kitchen windows. There they were, heads bent, pulled into the paper.

As he slid open the door to the shed, the dank pent-up air assaulted his senses. The lawnmower, smelling of dried sweet grass from last week's journey back and forth across the yard, took up most of the space in the middle of the small room. Then there were the dirt-covered garden tools—veritable instruments of torture if correctly applied to some unsuspecting passerby. He eyed them with a mixture of distrust and respect, the way one sometimes makes a mental note that a person, even though he might be evil, may be of some use later on, and as a result the information is filed in memory. Now the wave of nausea was becoming more intense. This was nothing new. It happened just this way every Sunday and this one was to be no different. He knew he would have to hurry in order to stay the flow of it, in order to counter it with something so that it didn't consume him.

It seemed that he was almost in a trance now. As he took out the cigarette and the matches, he barely noticed the nests of spiders in the corners underneath patio furniture, or the small insects picking their way across the floor of the shed. It was always this way, this strange feeling that came over him, and he was once again experiencing it as he lit the match and held it to the end of the cigarette. He drew in just enough breath to make sure the tobacco caught and then held it out. He thought to himself how amazing it was that the instrument of torture didn't really matter—it was the end result of pain that was the important thing. As he slipped the bottoms of his pajamas down, he viewed the many scars on his legs and lower abdomen. He thought to himself how he had enjoyed making these with the razor blades he had collected. What a shame that his parents had found out. Now they had hidden almost all dangerous objects around the house, not realizing that when someone wanted to inflict pain on himself, just about anything would do.

The nausea was now going full tilt. He knew he had to act fast in order to reverse its effect. He hadn't counted on this morning's search taking so long. He tried to locate an area on his thigh which wasn't already scarred by the cuts he had made previously. He also had to be careful to make sure it was high enough so that his parents wouldn't see it when he wore shorts. Before he touched the burning end of the cigarette to himself he thought about the effects that this self-inflicted torture had on his family. When his parents had first found out, denial had been the way to go. Then, after things really picked up, a therapist was consulted under the utmost secrecy. Of all things which he considered painful, having to go to his weekly sessions with the counselor or therapist or psychiatrist or whatever they called her, was the worst. He had now become an expert in lying, telling her what it was she wanted to hear, feigning that he no longer sought self-mutilation.

All of this he thought about as he took the burning cigarette between his forefinger and thumb. He tried to control his shaking hand, but the nausea was now too intense, and he felt that he might faint at any moment. As the living, breathing ash of the tobacco touched his flesh, his hand steadied and he tilted his head back and closed his eyes. The smell of burning skin made him light-headed, but the intense pain seemed not only to take that away, but the previous nausea as well. After burning himself a few more times, he extinguished the cigarette on the cement floor, flicking it into a small puddle of water which ran underneath a heap of broken flowerpots.

He would sit in the shed for another ten minutes and no more, waiting for the nausea to completely pass and for the smell of burning flesh to dissipate. He knew that before reentering the house—his life, the dreams, the insanity that only seemed sane when he was experiencing physical pain and not the mental anguish which followed him around so much of his life—he should bury the half-burned cigarette. He would have to retrieve it from the dark puddle he had sent it into. He thought he would choose some location that was secret and far away from the house. Some place his parents would never look. But instead, he decided to repossess the butt. He had another idea.

Having now picked up the remains of the cigarette, he began to peel away the layers of paper, fibers, and tobacco until it became nothing but a heap of indistinguishable materials, now harmless and inactive. The pieces were left scattered about the floor, blending in with the dirt, the grass clippings, the spider-webs.

As he sat there in the darkness—only a sliver of morning light making its way in through the rough-hewn wooden doors of the small building—he began to make out sounds of the other children in the neighborhood playing together. Three, four doors down. Was that the Hundly twins or the Babcocks that were making those noises, the peals of childish laughter, the squeals which were always a precursor to being tagged out or being caught in a game of hide-and-seek? He knew that he should be out playing with them, that he should return to their world and act as if nothing were wrong. And he knew that he would, in time, if only for a short while in order to disguise his secret life.

By lunch time, he would join in their celebration of childhood, matching them tag for tag, cunningly managing to escape detection while hiding behind a holly bush that no one had thought to use before, or by impressing them with his ability to change directions while running, even on a bed of slippery pine needles. He knew all the things that would make him popular with children his own age and he used them as often as he could, knowledgeable somewhere in the back of his mind that one day his set of social skills might fail him, but that for now at least, he could enjoy this game of hide-and-seek. And it was this game, so simple in its inception and handed down through the generations, that he found comfort in, for even if he were caught by a too-quick hand of some laughing school girl or the pre-adolescent tackle of one of his boyhood friends, he knew that the next time the games were played he would have thought of some alternative to their pursuits. He knew that in order to survive, he would be one step ahead of them, and so after a few more minutes of hiding in the shed, he carefully stepped out the door, silently reinstated the latch, and made his way back to his room where he would at least be safe until the next weekend.

CHRISTMAS COMES BUT ONCE A YEAR

Ollie Brandsnicker regarded the outside of the envelope with dread. It was the same thing every year during the first few weeks of December. He recognized his cousin's address from the ready-made return sticker, complete with miniature snowman and oversized snowflakes, and wondered what the mailman thought about the offending envelope. Midwest tacky. But then, this was New York, and they had probably seen a little of everything, just as he had his last ten years living in the city.

Ollie knew he would have to open the letter, but as always he dreaded the chore. After sorting through the rest of the mail (two bills, one letter that wasn't his, and two identical catalogs from a nationally recognized retail store that specialized in prosaic home furnishings), he finally acquiesced and tore into the moist weather-beaten envelope. As usual it wasn't a card that popped out, but rather the proverbial "Christmas letter" that he so feared. His cousin was given to sending these newsletters each year, confident that everyone enjoyed hearing about her latest fudge recipes and sanctimonious preaching. In the past, Ollie had thought that by not sending a card back or responding in any way, the letters would stop, but each season they arrived like the latest version of the flu.

He unfolded the letter. A gauche border of oversized pine cones and too-green holly assaulted his sense of good taste and it took a minute for his eyes to adjust. Then at the bottom he spotted the gold-leaf rendition of praying hands, complete with several gold stars surrounding them. Even without these hints he knew what to expect. His eyes made their way back up to the beginning of the letter.

> Your annual Christmas letter from Dan, Candy, Cody, Melody, and Diddly Brandsnicker!!!
>
> Well, it's that time of year again. We hope all of you are well and that this past year has been fruitful

and beneficial in the name of our Lord and Savior, Jesus Christ. And speaking of HIM, let us not forget that this season is about HIM and the fact that HE died for our sins. Praise HIM and HIS holiness, Amen.

Now, let's get down to what has happened in the past eleven months. First, let's take Melody, our youngest at thirteen years of age. She was VOTED most likely to win the giant chocolate bar at this year's spelling bee held in Guernesey City. Melody is EXTREMELY popular in her class, given the fact that she won the talent competition two years in a row with her version of "Memory" from *Cats*, even though the first year someone stole her costume and she was forced to perform dressed as a banana. She had participated in Lucille Prendergast's "Fruits on Parade" skit before intermission and there wasn't time to change even if we could have found her dress. While she only came in second place at the spelling bee (she won the snow globe) we're still proud of her and her Christian values. She told me after her near-miss to Guernesey City's Marsha Tellabandano (the first-place winner and a little too dark-complexioned to be calling herself Caucasian if you ask me), "Mom, look at how the Lord has blessed me. HE is so good, allowing me to win only second place. It must be that chocolate is the work of the devil. Praise HIM." We hope Melody continues with her Bible studies as she one day strives to be a professional Sunday school teacher, but hopefully without that banana costume!!!

Now, let's move on to Cody, our oldest and heir to the Brandsnicker fortune. As many of you know, Cody was quite a handful when he was younger, having been a Caesarean birth. I thought we'd never get his head out!! We still have videotapes of the blessed event, so if anyone wants one, just write to us with $5.60 for postage and we'll be happy to send it right along. We're happy to report that Cody has grown into quite a young man, having reached the height of 6'2" at the age of fifteen, and weighing over

200 pounds! He plays in the high school band where he sits last chair sousaphone, and we're confident that he will make something of himself someday as he is very interested in doing the Lord's work and is "spiritual leader" for the sousaphone section where he guides them in prayer before and after each half-time show. Cody is the FIRST PERSON in the history of Guernesey City to sit fourth chair sousaphone in the band! You go Cody!!!

Well, I guess it's time we got to Daddy Dan Brandsnicker. The first few months of last year were hard on Dan as he had a bad case of toenail fungus. We tried just about everything but the fungus just kept spreading to all of his toes until the ugly yellowed nails came completely off. Yuck, Daddy!!! Diddly, our Yorkshire terrier (actually he's part Chihuahua and part Pekinese), even found one in his food dish and brought it to us. Thanks Diddly! He's doing much better now (Dan, not Diddly) and we're thankful that after the prayer services held around his feet, delivered by the deacons at our church, that the fungus has completely disappeared. An additional prayer service is scheduled for February 6th of this year, just to be sure that the devil spores don't return, so mark your calendars! We know that if we trust in the LORD that HE will banish this awful fungus forever. Praise HIM! Other than that problem, Dan has been doing well at work, recently being promoted to Senior Assistant Manager of the frozen foods department at the Piggly-Wiggly. He replaced a rather un-Christian fellow who was reputed to be a homosexual with AIDS, and since we know that AIDS is God's vengeance on the sodomites, we can only assume that Dan was chosen to show the way of the LORD to all who work in food distribution.

Now here's the part I'm not very good at. This is where I have to talk about myself and all that I've done. I know the Lord says we should not brag, but I believe that others need to know of the good deeds performed throughout the year so that Satan doesn't get us down. So here goes.

The first month of the New Year I was elected chairperson for the Guernesey City Ladies Auxiliary for Handicap Ramp Installation (or GCLAHRI for short.) I know it sounds complicated but it really just involves making sure that all sidewalks are accessible to our less-blessed individuals. The only problem we had was with Blankenship's hardware on South Main. Mr. Blankenship refused to donate half of the cost of installation on the grounds that none of his customers were handicapped. After the Junior League picketed for several hours one Saturday he changed his mind. The prayer vigil outside didn't hurt any either, and once again GOD came to our aid. Shame on you, Charles Blankenship! We won't shop at your store anymore! After things calmed down I resigned my position as chairman (we only have three streets in town) and moved on to become Guernesey City's first woman to ever bake twelve cakes in one day, and all the same flavor! We've contacted Ripley's Believe It or Not, but so far they haven't called us back.

Well, I should sign off now until next year. Nothing much really happened to tell about in the rest of the family except that a cousin was nominated for some book award and a great uncle on mother's side posthumously won an award for discovering the cure for some disease (hope it wasn't AIDS!!!). But we know how that mundane stuff doesn't interest any of our friends. Until next year, remember to keep the LORD in your heart and remember that this season is in remembrance of HIM.

We LOVE you!!!!! GOD bless all.

Dan, Candy, Melody, Cody, and Diddly Brandsnicker

P.S. Come visit!

Christmas came and went that year after the family newsletter, and Ollie found himself consumed with life in Manhattan, forgetting about his family, and especially his cousin. He was working on a new collection of short stories and had just been named senior editor at one of the most prestigious magazines in the city, so his days were busy with things literary and not much thought was given to relatives or toenail fungus. The seasons melded together and before he knew what was happening, the weather turned cold once again with Christmas only a few weeks away.

Returning home from work one day, he fumbled his way to his apartment after retrieving the mail from the over-painted mailbox located in the lobby of his building. As the elevator carried him up, he shuffled through the fat stack of mail: Three Christmas cards (you could tell by the shape and coloration of the envelope, not to mention the return address—always from someone you hadn't heard from in a year); four catalogs, again from that national retail home furnishing chain; three misdirected postcards whose city and zip code didn't even match his own, and two magazines. But there was one more piece of mail in the equation. It was a letter-sized envelope with glitter snowflakes strategically positioned around the address. He knew before he opened it what it was going to say, but like someone who wants to watch open-heart surgery yet at the same time is sickened by the sight, he couldn't help himself, and tore into the glitter and overly feminine handwriting to get to the new information the letter contained.

> Greetings and a Merry Christmas from the Brandsnicker family! We're so blessed this year that we've thought about calling each and every one of you, but Dan seems to think we need to save money, so here's our contribution in print!!! All the better, I suppose, as we can now tithe more to the LORD for all he has done for us. So let's jump right in with what has been happening this past year!!!!!!!

We'll start with our oldest, Cody. He's now 6'2" and over 260 pounds! We're so proud of him and the fact that he's now this year's runner up for Guernesey City's hog-calling championship. Guess playing that sousaphone really paid off, huh, Cody! While he still sits last chair in the band, we have confidence that the LORD will bless him in other ways. Did you know Cody has size 13 feet!

Now for Melody, our youngest. As many of you know, Melody has had a problem with acne over this past year. We prayed about this and one day while I was doing dishes, the LORD'S image came to me in the reflection of the can opener. I knelt and prayed, and when I looked up I noticed that something was sticking out from the cabinet below the sink. On further investigation, I found boxes and boxes of band candy—a forbidden item in the Brandsnicker household. We knew Cody wasn't guilty as he was too busy practicing, so we questioned Melody even though she is not *in* the band. Well, to make a long story short, Melody has an addiction problem—to chocolate. We all knelt and prayed around the refrigerator and asked GOD to intervene and we're confident that Melody will lick this problem before our next letter to you all. We know that this is the LORD'S way of testing us and we accept it. We praise HIM and the problems HE has put in front of us.

On to Dan now. Well, Daddy Daniel is doing much better, having been promoted to Assistant Manager of Projects in shelf display at the Piggly-Wiggly. Evidently the area he was previously assigned to, benefited from his Christian example and we can only hope that no more homosexuals will be found in our food chains around the country. Dan's new manager is the nicest man who seems to have all the right values: a lovely wife, three adorable children, and two brand-new cars! We hope that the pressures of food display don't dent Dan and his boss's friendship!

A note about Diddly. He hasn't been feeling too well as of late and this year he has logged in over twelve hours of vet time. We're still not sure what's the matter with him, but we feel certain that the prayer blanket we ordered from TV will help. Thank you Pat Robertson!!!!!

And, as you all know, I always save myself for last. It breaks my heart to report that Ripley's has turned us down. It seems that some Satan-worshiping woman in California holds the record for the number of cakes baked in one day. Obviously the Brandsnickers—as well as the entire town of Guernesey City—are crushed, but we must persevere. This is just HIS way of telling me that I should move on to pies, I guess. At any rate, I've now been doing late-night volunteer work at the suicide hotline in the hope of reaching some storm-tossed person. With God's help I may be able to turn some lost soul around and point them in the direction of the LORD before it's too late! I did have one boy who was suicidal call me, and when I asked him "Why" he told me, after a long and anguished ordeal, that he was "gay." I know it was my duty to try and save this individual, but I felt the LORD intervening and I told him that he would be better off dead. He hung up so we'll never know if I got through to him or not. Praise the LORD for all his guidance!!!!!!

Praise HIM and all that HE stands for. LOVE to you all—The Brandsnickers!!!!!!!

Ollie folded the letter and put it in a drawer with the other correspondence from his relatives. As he did so, memories of his cousin came back to him, along with those languid and lackadaisical days in Missouri—his home state. His cousin had been just as odd then, with her sanctimonious faux-Christian values and underlying emotional greed. But it seemed she had gotten worse lately, gradually losing her grip on reality.

And she wasn't much to look at either. He remembered her flat-heeled shoes, her protruding abdomen, how she chain-sucked so many cigarettes that the skin around her lips had miniature gullies running down into her mouth. The woman had all the panache of a dog handler at the Westminster Dog Show. The only thing missing was the dog. But then she had Diddly.

As if these things weren't bad enough, Ollie remembered that she had often conspired with his mother, cooking up schemes to get rid of family pets and telling his teachers that he hated them, when in fact just the opposite was true. He had thought that somehow she would grow out of her attitudes, but they only seemed to fester like some great oozing sore that refuses to heal.

Ollie promised himself that he would never again open one of these letters, but after a year of traveling around the country on a book signing, and a meeting in Paris with one of his other cousins who was now a famous news journalist covering major events in the world, he forgot, and once again found himself standing in the vestibule of his building, sorting through his pile-up of mail after having been away for so long. The usual things were there: bills for electricity, telephone, rent. Then there were the magazines—even the ones he had cancelled. Then the letters from those magazines complaining that he hadn't paid the subscription even though his attorney had written a letter canceling them. There were now twelve catalogs from the retail outlet, and their rabbit-like reproductive capabilities were beginning to annoy him. Finally, there were the year's new phone books, tome-like and weighty with the names of millions of New Yorkers. Then Ollie saw it. The dreaded Christmas letter. This year's decoration was an angel stamp which had been freely applied to both sides of the envelope, the bottom of the angel's skirt forming the letters "PRAISE HIM!"

Ollie worked his finger at the open corner of the envelope and tore into it, tattering the edges so that they now resembled precariously attached pieces of confetti.

Merry CHRISTmas from the Brandsnickers!!!!!!!

It's Christmas once again at the Brandsnickers and we're glad to be able to share all of the past year's trials and tribulations with our friends and relatives.

To start off with, as many of you know, Dan has been working hard this year, staying late almost every night of the week and then some on weekends. It seems that his boss also works late and the two have developed quite a friendship. Once they even worked so hard that neither of them could drive home and they had to spend the night in some dump of a motel on Route 9! But all of that hard work has paid off since Dan is now Senior VP of Marketing and Sales! We're so proud of you Dan. You go boy!!!! Faith in our LORD and a strong desire to truly be a GOOD person really does make a difference.

Now, on to Melody. Many of you were unfortunate enough to see the front-page photograph of our youngest being arrested, in the *Guernesey City Daily*. Yes, she was wearing fishnet stockings, yes she had on black eye shadow, and yes she was in handcuffs. At first we were devastated. Then we found out the truth. When we met with Melody in her cell—the judge would not allow bail—we discovered that she had only been "posing" as a call girl in order to witness to those poor individuals from nearby Curby Ridge who insist on selling themselves to the depraved and Satanic-minded persons who call themselves Guerneseyites! We know the truth, Melody, and it's time everyone did. We're also happy to report that this youngest of ours, (fifteen now) has kicked the chocolate habit. The only withdrawal symptoms seem to be her dilated pupils and a slightly slurred speech pattern. But we know that she is doing well despite her previous addiction. Just the other day, she said to me, "Mom, the Lord has blessed me so (and at this point she wiped her nose with the overly long sleeve of her denim jacket), just look at all that HE's given me." I know that with the LORD's help Melody will continue to be a bastion of strength for us and our church. Praise GOD!!!

On a sad note, we're sorry to report that Diddly has become seriously ill. The doctor seems to think that some sort of fungus of the gums may be the culprit. We love and cherish our pet and WE WILL PRAY FOR YOU DIDDLY!!!!!!!!!

Now, about Cody. As you know he is seventeen, an age when the hormones start raging in our young people. We're confident that the two things he enjoys most—playing the sousaphone and praying—will lead him in the right direction. Just last Sunday, he led the singing in church with one hand while playing the sousaphone with the other. For those of you who don't know what a sousaphone is, it is the marching band version of the tuba and has a large flared bell which sticks upright. Still, as large as the instrument is, Cody has trouble getting "into" the thing. He's now 6 feet 2 inches tall and over 300 pounds!!! That's our boy!

Once again, it's my turn. Ah, to be the lucky mother of two delightful children and a loving and faithful husband. There is nothing more the LORD could have given me, with the exception of no Mexican neighbors. I don't mean to be a spoiled sport, but, as you know, most Mexicans are Catholic and these that we have living down the block are going straight to hell in my opinion. Unless you belong to our church, you don't stand a chance. But I won't dwell on these people. Hopefully, if I pray hard enough, the LORD will bless them and make their country economically viable enough for them to move back.

There's not much more to tell you folks this year. Dan's sister, Sally, came to visit after six months as a journalist, traveling for a major news corporation, and a nephew of mine who is only twelve just received a scholarship to the Juilliard School in New York. We can only pray that the heathens of other lands don't molest Sally and that New York doesn't corrupt any of my kin!!!!

Remember to dwell in the house of the LORD and praise HIM. In HIS name, we pray, AMEN!!!!!

Faithfully yours,

Candy, Dan, Melody, Cody, and Diddly

Ollie tried to forget about the letter as soon as possible. He hadn't spoken with his cousin in over ten years, yet she persisted in sending these letters. Forget about the content. Even her particular brand of style—if you could call it that—was irritating. The woman was well on her way to becoming nothing but a series of capital letters and exclamation marks.

But as usual, his hectic life in New York dictated that he forget the letter and move ahead, and so Ollie, consumed with the bustling season and the even more bustling new year, put aside not only the letter, but all thoughts of home and his relatives. Ollie had just finished another book and was preparing to have it sent to press, so most of the year was taken up with proofreading, editing, and meetings with his publisher. The year was filled with a plethora of other things as well: He gave a series of lectures in Russia and China on the state of the American novel, and had even run into one of his second cousins overseas. The cousin was now a Rhodes scholar and the two of them met in Istanbul for lunch, getting a chance to brush up on their Russian—they were fluent.

Back in the states, Ollie found time to work at a benefit for the homeless and become elected chairman for a committee to raise AIDS awareness. Still, it was a shock, as it always was, when Christmas rolled around and he opened his mailbox to a cascade of seasonal mail that spilled from it, restless and waiting to be opened.

The bounty was never-ending: There were no less than twenty-three catalogs from the same offending retail chain, and now not only were there magazines whose subscriptions he had cancelled, but there were duplicates of those subscriptions as well. This year's Christmas card pickings were slim: only three cards, all bearing—strangely enough—the same style and color of return address label, even though they were from different people, none of whom knew one another. Finally, he saw the most offending member of the pile, gingerly nestled between the last catalog and a notice to cut off his electricity—even though he had paid the bill, never been late, and had the cancelled check in hand.

He extracted the letter-sized envelope with the tips of his fingers, the way one might who is afraid the contents are radioactive. Carrying it this way into his apartment, he set it down on the hall table and began rummaging through the drawer, looking for the letter opener. It was as though he were going to perform surgery on the thing, for today he didn't feel like sticking his fingers into the loose end and working the casing open. He wanted something else to do the work.

Finally the letter was released into the open air of his apartment and he was reading.

Greetings from the Brandsnicker family!!!!!!!!!

Another year has come and gone and we're all still here. Well, all of us except one.

I don't want to start this Christmas letter off on a depressing note, but I feel I must get the bad news out up front. Diddly, our beloved Yorkshire Terrier, has died. On Friday, May 13th (an obvious bad omen because of the Satanic number 13), we carried our poor Diddly to the vet. He had stopped eating for several days and was wheezing through his nose. The vet insisted on doing exploratory surgery and when he opened up poor Diddly, he found exactly nine yellowish, hard, plastic-looking pieces of material. We can't imagine where he could have gotten such things and we have all been racking our brains to figure out just where this poor creature could have picked these up. The vet also looked into Diddly's nose and mouth and discovered that a fungus had infected his entire brain cavity, causing our poor little baby to have a bad case of dementia. That would explain his loss of bladder control and obsession with the toilet plunger in the powder room just off the kitchen. So it is with great sorrow that we mourn the passing of Diddly from this earth, but we know that the LORD will take care of his little withered body and we are thankful for that. See you in heaven, Diddly!!!!!!

Now, on a lighter note, our youngest, Melody, has once again been witnessing for the LORD. It seems that she was arrested one balmy Friday night while attempting to sell drugs to an undercover police officer. Of course, as she explained to us, she was only trying to find out if the officer was really going to take the drugs so that she could then witness to him and convince him to turn to our LORD. Now, the police don't believe her story, but Dan and I stand by her and as always, we KNOW that her intentions were honorable. And we feel that it is only a matter of time before the rest of the town comes around to our way of thinking. You go Melody!!!!!!!

Our oldest, Cody, is a senior in high school this year and it looks as though he may be a senior once again next year. His grades were so bad the first half of the year that he will have to attend next year AGAIN to graduate. We know this is just the LORD's way of testing us and that's just fine! If the LORD sees fit that Cody should stay around to lead the sousaphone section in prayer one more year, then so be it! We don't really blame Cody for his past performance in school, because last October Cody had an attack of appendicitis and was in the hospital for three days. Mary Lou, our beloved florist in Guernesey, sent him the cutest arrangement of flowers with small sousaphones stuck in it. Thank you Mary Lou!!!!!!

And now for the really good news. As many of you know, Dan has been spending more and more time away from home because of his work. So much so, in fact, that he has had to move into a house just five minutes away from his office. Yes, he has had to leave his family temporarily in order to more closely witness to those in food distribution services. It seems that his boss is also living in the home. So dedicated are these two men, that we know the LORD will bless them with goodness and charity, and that one day they will return to their respective homes to be with their families. Neither Dan's boss's wife or I have seen either of our husbands, but we know that they are working hard at making the world a safer place for food distribution. Keep those frozen peas safe, Dan!!!

Once again, it's my turn. What can I say? This year has been a roller coaster of emotions for all of us, what with the price of gasoline going up and our children becoming better and better CHRISTIANS day by day. The only real drawback has been the NEGRO family who has moved in down the street. Now, I'm not being racist, but the Bible says that the races should not mix and I believe that our LORD was referring to neighborhoods as well as marriages when he said this.

Other than that, about the only thing new in the family was my sister's boy, Rudolph, who got some type of scholarship that has to do with roads or something. He's going to England for a year and then on to Russia after that. Better him than me as I do NOT like to travel and I am NOT a Communist sympathizer. You all have a good rest of the year and remember to keep the LORD most HOLY as HE is the WAY.

Always spreading GOD's WORD,
Candy, Dan, Melody, and Cody

"That's it," thought Ollie. "I'm never opening another one of these things again." But the year flew by, and distracted by an aunt and uncle's death and an all expense-paid trip to Frankfurt to see a second cousin conduct a series of orchestra concerts there, he forgot about the letter and its plebian contents. Toward the end of September another of his cousins (it was, after all, a large family) moved from Atlanta to New York to become the president of one of the major stock exchanges in the city. There was an elegant party thrown at the Waldorf, resplendent with the governor of New York, the mayor of the city, and no less than twelve major celebrities. So it was understandable that Ollie forgot, because of the recent festivities as well as the skyrocketing sales of his latest book, his promise not to read the letters from his cousin, and found himself tearing into the fir-scented envelope while standing at his mailbox. He was just about to extract the letter when he realized something was different. No catalogs. Not one. He bent lower to look more closely inside the square metal container that held his mail, but there was nothing. He was just straightening up, experiencing an elation he had never known before, when he heard the Puerto Rican doorman's voice calling to him from the other side of the echoing, tiled lobby.

"Yo, Ollie B," the man verbally threw at him while working his foot at something under his desk. "Dis here ting's for jew," and with that the doorman pushed a medium-sized box out and into the middle of the floor. Ollie met the box halfway and was bending to pick it up. He scanned the label but couldn't make out who or where it was from. "Probably something for Christmas from one of the relatives," he thought as he carried it, along with the other mail, up to his apartment. Setting the box down, he used the sharp edge of his door key to score the top and sides. The receptacle was so packed with its contents that the minute he had released the tape which was holding the thing together it virtually exploded. The box was filled with catalogs, their covers showing earth-toned sofas and draperies, and there were now a good twenty or thirty scattered on the floor, with at least a hundred more still inside. And all from the same national retail chain that had been sending the things all along.

Ollie groaned and swept them to the side so that he wouldn't slip on them. Then he turned his attention to the Christmas letter with the morbid curiosity that one reserves for daytime television shows, and began to take in what had last happened to that particular section of the Brandsnicker family.

A Christmas Greeting on the LORD's birthday . . . From the Brandsnicker family . . .

This year's Christmas letter is tinged with sadness, and I promise I will not dwell on the unfortunate events of the past eleven months, but as many of you know, our oldest, Cody, was killed in an unfortunate accident this past October. I will recapitulate for those of you who are not aware of the entire saga. Being the good CHRISTIAN that Cody was, he was in the middle of leading the sousaphone section in prayer during the most important game of the season when the unfortunate event occurred, so we KNOW that it was GOD'S will and would never question OUR LORD further on the matter. For those of you who were not at the football game between Guernesey City High and Cleaton Central (Guernesey 40, Cleaton 2—Yeah Guernesey City Bob Cats!!!!) I will explain.

As many of you know, the sousaphone section sits on the top row of the stadium when the band is seated, playing for our beloved Bob Cats. Because the bell of the sousaphone is extremely large, it sticks up quite a bit above the chain-link fence that protects our beloved children from falling over the back of the stadium and into Jerry's Tire and Rim Replacement Center. The *Guernesey City Daily* reported that there were over sixty-five people in the stadium when the horrible accident took place—the one in which Deeter McRantay attempted his now famous pass (that boy has some throwing arm, let me tell you) and was tackled a mille-instant before, skewering his aim so that the ball flew sideways into the stadium.

It seems that Murphy's Law was in order that night, for at the very instant Cody and his adored sousaphone section stood up for prayer, the football flew directly into the large bell of Cody's instrument. The impact of such a powerful throw (Deeter now has a scholarship to State University), accompanied by the fact that Cody was somewhat unsteady on his feet (6'2" and over 475 pounds), caused our oldest to topple over the chain-link fence and onto the roof of Jerry's. The sousaphone, miraculously, was intact, but alas, our poor Cody was killed instantly in the fall. The roof to Jerry's will be repaired shortly and we know that the LORD will provide us with enough funds to fight the lawsuit. I would like to thank the many fellow Christians for their prayers and thoughts over these past troubling months and would especially like to acknowledge Charles Blankenship of Blankenship Hardware for his moral and spiritual support. As many of you know, Charles has been living with me since the accident as he and his wife are in the process of getting a divorce. Charles and I have made our peace with each other since the ugly incident involving curb remodeling in front of his lovely new store on Main Street. His guidance and insight into human suffering is remarkable and I could not get along without his undying CHRISTIAN values and his faith in the LORD.

Thank you Charles Blankenship for all you've done for my family. To show my support to his lovely soon-to-be ex-wife, Helen, I made her my famous crabmeat Louis casserole (from the recipe out of the Junior League cook book—$8.95 plus shipping, see Mrs. Bluewaart at Sipsy's River Café for details.) And Helen, if you get this letter before the 25th, I need my FIRE KING DISH BACK!!!

Now, on to the rest of the group. As many of you know, Melody has been witnessing extensively to many in the area, the latest group of which is the "Goths." Melody has even taken to PIERCING several dozen of her body parts in an attempt to "get in" with this Satanic crowd in order to fully witness to them about their abominable life-style. Just the other day she said to me, "Mom, look at how the LORD has blessed me. He's allowed me to witness to PROSTITUTES, drug addicts and even the Satan worshipers. I'm so glad I can tell others about HIM." Our youngest is truly an inspiration and it is wonderful that she gets along so well with Charles, our hardware man, and doesn't resent him for living with us. I praise GOD that he has blessed me with such a loving and understanding child. Charles is still trying to get back on his feet emotionally since the breakup with his wife, but I know that with the LORD's help that particular journey will be one of spiritual nourishment.

Well, we should discuss Dan now. For the last two years now, Dan and his boss have been living together so that they can work more extensively on "refining and developing" our nation's food distribution delivery and display services. So great is their zeal for what they do that they now travel around in matching outfits and have even adopted the same HAIRCUTS!!! You go boys!!!! It's so nice to see Dan finally coming into his own—he's now the President of Display and Pricing!!! And his boss is such a good CHRISTIAN man. This past year he took Dan on a trip to Key West and San Francisco, and gave him a solid gold watch for all of his years of service and devotion. I truly thank GOD for this blessing. We wish you well, Dan, and please know that you are loved by your family.

Let's see . . . who do we have left. Oh, yes!!! Me!!!! As many of you know, I DO NOT like to brag about my accomplishments, but I will just this once. As reported on the front page of the *Guernesey City Daily*, I won the fifth annual Guernesey City

POTHOLDER making championship. Now, I know there are those out there who said that because Charles Blankenship's ex-wife was in the hospital with food poisoning that I really didn't have any competition, but let me tell you, I worked and PRAYED HARD for that first-place award and I aim to keep it!!!!

Just a word about the rest of the family. My first cousin, Richard, was recently named President of one of those big companies in New York City—I can't remember the name, but they have something to do with stocks or something—and my sister Eunice's boy, Harold, is now conductor of an orchestra in Germany. Again, the city he's in is one of those new-fangled names that I can't even pronounce. Thank GOD I live in the U. S. of A!!!!!! My brother had a triple by-pass and both of my parents were killed by a drunk driver last July, but other than that not much has happened.

Signing off now with GOOD CHRISTIAN LOVE for all,

Me, Dan, Charles, and Melody.

"Well," thought Ollie, "at least she got the part about her parents dying accurate." He wasn't going to swear off reading these letters anymore. If he couldn't remember to throw them away, then it was his own fault. Besides, he might be able to do something with them someday—make something out of them.

The year passed much like the others. Ollie had another book published and each week it climbed higher and higher on the bestseller lists, finally making it to number one. Sometime around the last of November, just after Thanksgiving, Ollie was returning home when he noticed the headlines of a rather infamous newspaper—one that usually claims some movie star is dying or that aliens now live in the White House. He couldn't make out the picture of the baby on the front of the paper, but the headline was unmistakable. "GUERNESEY CITY WOMAN TO GIVE BIRTH TO NEW MESSIAH! IMMACULATE CONCEPTION THE CULPRIT!" Ollie didn't give it much thought until a week later when he opened yet another of his cousin's Christmas letters.

> It's a MIRACLE. That's all that can be said about it!!! PRAISE the LORD on HIGH!!!!
>
> Our beloved daughter, Melody, is scheduled to give birth to a BABY!!!! And here's just part of the amazing story: The doctor says the delivery is scheduled for DECEMBER 25TH!!!!!!!!!!!!!!!!!!!!!!!!!!!!!!!!!
>
> That's right! It wasn't enough that Melody came up PREGNANT out of thin air, but now this is truly a sign from HIM that the second MESSIAH is on his way. I will admit, at first I was skeptical when Melody told me she was pregnant, but after questioning her, I realized that she was telling the truth when she said that she had never experienced INTIMATE relations with a man. And as I thought about it, I realized that she had to be telling the truth. For the past year, Melody has rarely left the house, choosing to spend almost all of her time with Charles under his excellent CHRISTIAN tutelage. So you can see that this MIRACLE of birth which is to take place at the end of this month is exactly like Mary's when she gave birth to Jesus!!!!!!
>
> There were those in olden days who thought that MARY had experienced the "love of a man" and become "with child," but as we know now, it was Immaculate Conception, JUST LIKE MY MELODY!!!!!!
>
> Of course, we will be naming the baby JESUS and I've already bought the cutest "starter set" of carpenter toys from HOME DEPOT for the little tyke! This will be the best Christmas EVER!!!!!!!

I could go on and on about this MIRACLE birth, but the LORD is telling me that I need to spread more of the good news of our family, so here goes . . .

Dan and his boss have now moved to San Francisco where they can better "facilitate management" of the FOOD industry. I didn't even know that San Francisco was the food capital of the world!!!!! I do miss him terribly, but I know that he is doing the LORD's work and that his boss is such a good CHRISTIAN man that nothing can stand in their way. You go boys!!!!!!! I did see Dan one time before he left for the Coast. My, that man of mine has really shaped up!! You should see how fit and TAN he is now that he and his boss have been working out regularly. And their house!!!! Oh, my gosh! I only got to see the inside this time as they had it up for sale. Dan must be truly doing well as the inside was filled with antiques and priceless works of art. THE LORD HAS TRULY BLESSED THEM!!!!!!!!!!!!!!!!!!

Many thanks to all our friends and neighbors who have donated money for Cody's funeral EXPENSES that were incurred last year. At the time, we had no idea that the specially built coffin would COST so much, especially because of Cody's size and the fact that he had requested to be buried with his instrument, but with GOD's help in this matter, we have finally achieved our money goals. Thanks to all in the Guernesey City area!!!!!!!

On a sad note, Helen, beloved ex-wife of Charles, and mother to two adorable children, has finally succumbed to the awful bout of food poisoning she contacted last year. The coma was long and hard on us all, but after months of suffering she is with our LORD. Praise HIM and all that HE has done for this poor unfortunate family. Just a note before I sign off for the year. My sister's boy won some type of piano competition (Chi-kow-ess-keee?—I'm not sure how you spell the darn thing but it was in Russia) and my first cousin living in New York City has had another book published. It was on some best-seller list for the past six months. Wish he'd get a REAL job!!!!!!!!!!

GOD BLESS you all and keep us in your prayers!!!!!!!! Until next year!!!!!

Ollie stood there in the lobby of his apartment building, where the mailboxes were located, and read the entire thing. He was so distracted by the letter that he hadn't noticed the pile of boxes that almost blocked the way to the elevators.

"Ralphie?" Ollie questioned toward the front desk. "What are these boxes for?" The despondent and diffident doorman responded with his usual shortness: "Dose are for jew."

Ollie looked at the address on one of the boxes. They were indeed for him. Then he saw the company logo and name.

"Oh, no. No, no, no, no. Ralphie, you tell whoever delivered these to take them back. I'm through with this thing. I don't know what's going on here, but have whoever brought them take them back."

"Whas dee matter?" asked Ralphie in his thick Spanish accent, "you doan like mail order?"

"I like mail order fine," said Ollie, "I just don't like three thousand catalogs, and now they're coming in boxes?"

Ralphie just shrugged

Ollie made his way into the elevator and pressed the button for his floor. Once inside his apartment, he relinquished the letter to the drawer of the hall table, along with the copied newspaper clipping and front-page headline that had been included with the Christmas letter—the clipping showing the supposed "new Messiah." They were beginning to pile up, these letters that appeared each year, and now the drawer was overflowing with accounts of Cody and Melody and Diddly, and everyone else.

Ollie's new year was filled with book signings, lectures, and a three-month vacation he treated himself to at the end of the summer, and as usual all thoughts of relatives and sousaphones slipped his mind. Sometime around October his agent called and reminded him that he owed one more short story to one of those few magazines that still published them—always wedged inconspicuously somewhere in between the latest dieting fads and some political article. Ollie managed to stall for time and get the publication to print his story in February. After all, he couldn't very well complete it until the last bit of information came into play, and that wouldn't happen until December.

The Christmas season this year was different for Ollie, for he tore into the bright red-and-green envelope with great anticipation, totally ignoring the small Christmas-tree-shaped-pieces of glitter that spilled onto the floor, eager to read what would he hoped would be the final note in this twisted Muzak symphony of sounds one called family. The rest of the mail could wait. He stood there in the dim light of his apartment lobby, taking in everything, finding that he was now addicted to the information, as if by reading the letters over the years he had become so accustomed to them that he found it irritating to have to wait an entire year for the next installment.

> Greetings from our new and modified CHRISTIAN family . . .
>
> Well, this first year of living with the Messiah has been a blessing. Little Jesus will be exactly ONE YEAR OLD this coming December 25th. We're so proud that GOD picked our little Melody to be the vessel to carry this infant and now, just watching him suckle at her teat fills me with enormous pride. So much pride, in fact, that we have contacted a local taker of portraits to make a large six-foot by four-foot print of the BREAST-FEEDING. I picked out Melody's dress from Wal-Mart myself and you should see the ruffles. It is an ORGANDY number with small prints of birds and bees all over it!!! Actually all of you WILL get to see the dress and the photograph of her breast-feeding baby Jesus as we plan to mass-market the picture and sell it on the Home Shopping Network for $499.95 apiece. We're taking special orders now, and if you're a relative or friend you can

get in on the ground floor price of only $399.95 until this coming March—all others will have to wait!!!!! We're so excited about this opportunity that the LORD has given us. At least TWO PERCENT of the proceeds will be given to Blankenship's Hardware and another two percent to the 700 Club. Well, that's enough about Jesus and me for now, as I should tell you what has been happening in the rest of the family's life, so here goes:

Melody is breast-feeding—we've covered THAT. And Charles Blankenship will be settling comfortably into a new home with Melody and baby in the next several months. Thank the LORD for a man with honorable intentions. It is so good of Charles to move in with Melody and take care of her and baby Jesus. I only hope that one day he sees fit to remove the RESTRAINING order he and Melody have placed against me as I would love to be a part of OUR SAVIOR's life at some point. I know that Charles has the best intentions and I will wait patiently like the faithful SERVANT OF GOD that I am. Praise HIM!!!!!!!

Now, about my husband Dan. A few months ago I received a notice from Dan's attorney, asking me for a divorce. I JUMPED for joy that the LORD was testing me in this way!!!! Of course I decided to give him the divorce he sought as it would only make my life more miserable and as we all know, you must SUFFER incredibly in order to be a good CHRISTIAN. THANK YOU JESUS (the first one) for this great OPPORTUNITY to serve you and all that you stand for!!!!!!!! I know that if I am PATIENT and do the LORD's work, that he will BLESS me and eventually RETURN Dan to me and allow me to see my GRANDBABY JESUS. PRAISE HIM AND ALL THAT HE STANDS FOR!!!!!!!!!!!

Until next YEAR!!!!!!!!!!!
Candy

Ollie folded the letter and smiled to himself. He was completely lost in thought now, thinking about how he would position this last letter into the short story he was writing. And he was so lost in thought that he never noticed the brown UPS truck with its burly driver who climbed down from the cab and made his way to the back of the vehicle. He never noticed the large wooden skid containing the fifty boxes of catalogs which the driver had left on the sidewalk, just outside the front door to his building—never noticed them, that is, until the driver had gone and it was too late.

A FOREST OF GREEN

Vertical beams of morning sun filtered down through the verdant cathedral of trees and onto the path he was taking. As he moved through the forest, the shafts of sunlight became momentarily disoriented, interrupted by the long, elegant tree trunks. The beams of light would then regain their footing on the velvety foliage which carpeted the forest floor, their momentary occlusions adding to the overall effect—light streaming in through some great church window.

It seemed that at age forty-two he was beginning to notice the world around him more—this light, the flora, the colors, all of which seemed to bound out at him now with unexpected speed, like some pop-up boxed-in clown, released by one-too-many turns of the handle. He was beginning to notice all things in life, in the forest, in the world, that is, except for his manner of dress.

Today he had chosen one of the many flannel shirts and chinos he possessed. His best friend had criticized him earlier that morning for his careless attire, commenting on his tenacious selection of sameness each day. But it didn't matter. It wasn't as if there were multitudes of people around. It wasn't as if he had to interact with the world, or even a handful of people. And it was probably because of this lack of human contact that he was paying so much attention to his surroundings.

He noticed the moss-covered path before him, stretched out like a smooth green carpet, the hills and dales of it becoming another country altogether. Something was comforting about the solitude of the forest. Giant tree roots pushed themselves upward from the peaty loam underneath the velvet, their graduated shapes resembling a miniature mountain range in some far-off land—China; Tibet. Green growths of lichen and moss could easily have been thick forests containing tigers, exotic birds, and tribes of yet undiscovered natives—their customs rife with inexplicable and bizarre rituals. He imagined medicinal cures; medicines prepared out of ground animal skulls; fantastic potions made from small amphibians caught in a nearby stream; self-mutilations for the purpose of removing evil spirits. All of this he thought about as he silently made his way down the gently curving path. The mist that had fallen earlier made everything fresh-green, and this, along with the fact that the monochromatic landscape was comforting to him, made him start even more when he realized there was a small inanimate object buried near the edge of the path among a tussle of ferns. He stopped to bend down, taking his hands out of his pockets for the first time.

It seemed that he stared at it forever, attempting to make out what the object was, the way children lie awake at night trying to figure out what certain shapes are in their rooms. A pile of clothes on a chair turned at a strange angle could easily become some horrible monster holding its breath, waiting for you to fall asleep, hoping that you would give up the quest of analyzing its shape so that it could all the more easily devour you. The process of making sense out of the objects could take twenty or thirty minutes, the result usually being that before you knew what was happening, you had fallen back into dreamland and the monster had failed to materialize. Nevertheless, you had buried the blankets firmly around your neck in the event that the creature tried to drink your blood or sever your head from your frail twelve-year-old body.

So it was with this scrutiny that he observed the object now before him. It wasn't that it was so out of place in color, but that it seemed to be made up of an unusual degree of unconnected elements. This, accompanied by the fact that it was half covered by a sprig of club moss which hung over it like some pliable, protecting claw, made it all the more difficult to analyze.

Bending lower he summoned enough courage to stick his hand into the crisp foliage which nurtured the edge of the path. It wasn't that he was afraid of surprising some small animal or snake in the process; indeed, he had noticed that the landscape was almost entirely void of wildlife. There was not a bird sound anywhere, and as he had walked through the woods he had heard no rustling of leaves made by small creatures which are usually eager to escape into the confines of a secure tree trunk or underground thicket at the sound of a passing human. No, his hesitation was because he wasn't entirely sure he wanted to know what the object was. He wasn't sure he wanted to disturb it. Or have it disturb him.

Before his brain could decide what to do, his hand had firmly grasped the entity (his sense of touch was already trying to make sense of it) and he was gently pulling it from the moist earth as if extracting a molar from the mouth of some sleeping anesthetized giant. He thought that if he pulled with just the right amount of care and speed, the giant wouldn't notice its loss and would wake up in the morning with only an inexplicable modicum of soreness to his jaw.

The object seemed to free itself after a moment. Now, with the little help he had given it, it was grasped firmly in his hand. Small pieces of earth clung to its sides. There was a small black hole in the green forest floor blanket now, its tattered edges looking like a flesh wound which would take time to heal. He mashed the edges of moss down with his foot, the effect being inadequate since the object had occupied more space than the extant moss was willing to cover.

He had extracted a doll's head, inert and lifeless, having been removed sometime in the past from its Victorian body. He turned it over, looking into the deep hollow neck which he imagined holding innumerable secrets. A small innocuous spider (the only sign of life he had seen today) crawled out and over the pouting lips of the porcelain head, gingerly making its way through the cracked and patina-covered landscape that had once been a face. As it moved methodically, like a monk on some far-off pilgrimage to a place of worship it wasn't sure even existed, it was as if the creature was drawing attention to the facial attributes of the head. There was the white ceramic flesh, now aged and worn, flaked away from the surface of the head, making the stunning blue eyes which were completely intact all the more prominent. The eyes seemed to have been painted with a heavier glaze than the rest of the face and they, along with the good six inches of soft brown hair, were the only elements of the head that were intact. The object seemed to have occupied this spot for some time. Even so, the hair was in relatively good shape considering the object's location and surrounding climate.

He carefully placed a forefinger into the neck opening, hoping it only contained one spider. The moist, cool bisque of the unglazed inside felt comforting—a momentary refuge from a hostile world, this dark and dank inner chamber. He wondered if the child who had owned the doll had performed the same exercise. He wondered how the doll's head had come to be separated from the body. Had it been torn off in an angry confrontation over which cakes to serve with tea, or had there been an unusually hostile disagreement with some teddy bear or juggling clown? Perhaps another doll, jealous of its white lace Victorian dress, had purposely and with premeditation, planned the demise of this one, completely unaware of the emotional scars the act would inflict on the owner.

He wondered what a child would have been doing this deep into the woods anyway, this far from civilization. He imagined the cries of the youngster, wrestling to free herself from the firm grip of her mother, desperately pleading to take flight so that she could search the forest floor for that most important and defining attribute of the toy, for the head is everything when it comes to a doll. You could have just about any body underneath the velvets and lace, but the entire history and personality of the doll was in the face, the head, the color of the hair, the eyes.

He stared at it now, resting in his hand like a lifeless bird. It was dirty and old. Perhaps the owner had some communicable disease such as smallpox or cholera. After all, it was impossible to tell exactly who had owned it and when. The doll's head appeared to be from some earlier era—perhaps 1918 or before. The entire family could have succumbed to the great flu epidemic and certain germs might still be concealed within the crackled face and matted hair. He wished now that he hadn't touched the innermost recesses of its cranium.

The spider, the thought of some disease, and the fact that this remnant of childhood looked extremely unclean, led him to hold the head by the hair as he walked along the path. He was aware that the head seemed to be getting heavier as he strode along. By the time he reached a hairpin turn in the forest road, it seemed to weigh a good eight pounds, even though at first its weight had been equal to that of a full pack of cigarettes. But it was only a doll's head and it certainly hadn't changed size. Still, he felt like Salome holding the head of John the Baptist as he made his way through the wood.

It seemed that he walked for an hour or more before finally coming upon the stream. As he approached the edge of the water, he almost leaned over to see his reflection. Then something caught him and pulled him back, allowing him only to view the stream from a few feet away.

Loose clumps of bright algae glowed in hair-like masses deep within the water. He noticed the similarities of the doll's hair to the algae. Should he drown the small object with its sea sisters or save it for his cabin which was now within sight, a mere twenty yards from where he was standing? He opted for survival of the head instead of relegating it to a watery grave and continued on. As he entered his cabin—nothing more than a flimsy collection of boards and nails—he decided that the doll's head was just what his space needed. Besides, it was the first female companionship he had experienced in months.

While he had a best friend who came to see him—either that or they met near the edge of the woods at the border of the property where his friend's farm stopped and his property began—he missed certain aspects of his former life. The decision to remove himself from society had been a painful one. There had been other options, but he hadn't wanted to explore them. It was as if he had, in some twisted but logical way, been given what he needed, and now, instead of trying to rectify his shortcomings, he simply acquiesced to them.

He placed the head on the small shelf next to the only window of the cabin. He drew back the curtain of red gingham and let the sun filter into the room. Dust swirled in the light, seemingly not wanting to land on anything in particular.

As he washed his hands in the antique basin, he raised up to see himself in the mirror. It didn't matter how many times it happened, it was always a shock. He had gotten away from society for this very reason. He was tired of people's reaction to him, and now he was reacting to himself, guilty of the same thing he had accused others of. Why had he brought this broken piece of mirror into the cabin; yet another item confiscated from the forest floor? Was it some sort of self-torture he reveled in? Perhaps it was his way of trying to accept what had happened.

He gripped the broken edge of the mirror with his right hand, thinking he would fling it across the room and be done with the discomfort, but something made him hold on to it. It was as if he wanted the pain, the truth; as if he wanted the process of mental healing to begin.

With the mirror in his right hand, he gently stroked his face with his left, feeling the deep gullies and scars which now made up what was left of his features. He no longer felt sorry for himself. After all, it had been his own stupidity that had caused him to fire the shotgun before he placed the barrel in his mouth. He had wanted to end his life because of an intense emotional pain, and now he was forced to deal with an even more intense self-loathing.

The surgeons had done a remarkable job, replacing what they could with bone and tendon taken from other parts of his body, but he was still a damaged man, disfigured to the point where he could no longer remain a part of society.

As his hand traced the now sunken left side of his visage—the hollow eye socket, the grimace of teeth showing like a sick, childish grin—he marveled at his ability to see the torn, mangled flesh and not suffer disgust. It was after all, only himself. It was his own creation—a mass of bone and muscle and ligaments of his own doing. Perhaps that was the reason he had rescued the mirror. Deep down, some part of him knew that he would have to accept what he had done and come to terms with it.

He thought how ironic it was that of the limited objects he had chosen to bring into his cabin, one had been a mirror. And now he was again looking into its deep, flat pool at the grotesque face of a man, at the remnant of himself. What a strange journey it had been up to this point. He had become physically maimed by his own hand in order to find his spiritual self. Someone had once told him that there was no such thing as an accident. If that were the case, some part of him had intentionally manipulated the shotgun blast not to kill, but only to disfigure. Some part of him had sensed that his time wasn't up, that what he thought was the final burning out of ideas and relationships was nothing more than one door closing and another opening, and that what he had perceived to be a slowing down, an emotional dying, wasn't the end at all, but merely the beginning.

As he lay down on the narrow cot that was the room's only furniture, he tried to focus on the narrow strips of sky that showed through the badly patched roof. Clouds moved silently in and out of the asymmetrical openings, and in the distance the hum of a single-engine propeller plane droned like some remote mechanical insect.

It was some time later that he became aware his lips were moving, forming invisible words that were projected upward toward these slim blue openings. In his mind he could see them, these words as they floated toward the azure spaces above him, slowly making their way toward the apertures. He watched them for some time as they hovered near the ceiling before escaping like a child's toy balloon set free to discover the rest of the universe. And he watched them until his eyelids grew heavy and sleep overtook him—a welcomed dinghy, ferrying him slowly to a world of quiet and peacefulness.

CROOK

One

The Jell-O perched precariously on the plebian stainless steel spoon that the nursing home supplied. You would have thought that with both of us holding the eating implement, the wiggly substance would have been a little more stable. But I suppose that was too much to ask given the present circumstances. My aunt and I regarded the transparent red cubes with the same disdain: she, because her mind no longer recognized the dessert, and me, because I knew that the nursing home had probably given her the same thing to eat every day for the last six months.

"Come on, Nelle," I said, "just one more bite." I heard myself saying these words, but my heart was only half into the task. I knew that it was an uphill battle. My Aunt Vernelle had been in the Moulton, Alabama, nursing home now for almost a year, and her condition had deteriorated to such an extent that the nascent babblings which first accompanied her arrival had been reduced to blank stares with only the occasional light coming from her pupils when some word or phrase made its way through. And it was this momentary light, this spark of recognition that was at once painful and joyous when it did finally arrive. It was the one thing that I lived for on these visits. It had happened previously once or twice, but you could see it go as quickly as it had come, slipping away like some person-less canoe on determined river rapids. You could reach out your hand and try to hold on to it, but in the end it was no use—the thing was gone, down river where hopefully someone would find it and bring it back to its owner, if not in one piece, then at least recognizable enough to recall what the original item looked like. It was as if, on those rare instances, I could see her the way she used to be, the way she was before this disease took her memories, her dreams, and her life away.

Nelle had been diagnosed with Alzheimer's and relegated to this home by her son Jules—my cousin. It had to be done, as there was no other choice. Nelle's husband had died years earlier and now there were very few of us left in the family. Jules was living in Texas at the time she moved into the home, and other than his trip back to Alabama to place her there, was too far away to care for her. But that had been permanently remedied when cousin Jules got in a nasty fight at a bar in Houston and was shot dead by three men in a pickup truck. They sped off into the humid Texas night, the police never making any arrests. In a way I suppose it was for the best that it happened after Vernelle's encampment at the home, at a time when she wasn't sure what was going on. I tried to break the news to her when it occurred, along with the help of one of my cousins on my father's side, but as with most things, the meaning just didn't filter through, and Nelle was left the way she arrived—blank and distant. I was lucky enough to visit her every now and then, making my own difficult trip from New York once or twice a year, hoping to find some remnant of my slowly disappearing family—a family that had lived almost exclusively in northern Alabama.

The nursing home in Moulton was nicer than most, and the few remaining family members felt that Nelle would be well taken care of there. Besides, there seemed to be an inordinate number of Alzheimer's cases at the facility and we figured that since it was so popular with that crowd, the staff must know what they're doing. People in that area of the country were well acquainted with the effects the ailment could have on their relatives, and so there was a little extra care given to those who had slipped their own mental grasps, even if they weren't a member of your immediate family. A sort of "There but for the grace of God, go I," kind of thing.

Now, I guess you should know a little about Moulton, Alabama, since it is not only where the nursing home is, but also the closest town to where my Aunt Vernelle spent her entire life. It's not exactly the most cosmopolitan center of the world, but then that's what most people who live there like about it. To know the town and surrounding county isn't necessarily to love it. It's something that gets into your blood though, and while I never expected to have any sentimental attachment to it, I found myself ruminating over the time I had spent there as a child, visits to relatives, and most of all, my Aunt Vernelle who had lived her entire life in this one county, in this one town, and in the one and only house she had ever known after getting married in 1945. With the brief exception of a one-week honeymoon to Florida, Nelle had never been out of the county of her birth.

Moulton is a small place, situated in northern Alabama. It is the county seat of Lawrence County, but don't let that lead you astray. It is by no means a large town, even by Southern standards. The land surrounding Moulton and making up Lawrence County is a combination of deep-plowed furrows of cotton and beans alternating with thickets of tangled woods. The smaller towns (if they can even be called towns) surrounding Moulton are even more rural than the county seat, and they all tend to think of "M" town as the big city.

Even though this was Alabama, decades ago, by my recollection as a child there was very little in the way of racial turmoil in the area. It seemed to me at the time that everyone was white. Any disturbances over race usually happened in one of the nearby counties, or places like Decatur, Huntsville, or Birmingham. That's not to say that there were no people of color in the area, but rather that because of the sparseness of the population and the fact that houses could be miles apart, one wasn't apt to run into the same problems that could be encountered in enclaves that possessed a fire department, a post office, or a bank. Lawrence County, for the most part, was extremely rural.

From time to time there was news of some Indian burial mounds that had been discovered, and even word that the Negro son of a sharecropper's family had won a medal in the Olympics in Germany in 1938, but in this part of the country it was just considered something on the fringe and nothing much came of it. For the most part, the area around my Aunt Vernelle's home was strictly white. Strictly white and strictly poor. It wasn't that the people of the area didn't try or that they were lazy, but rather that the Great Depression in the 1930s had set a tone and pace for the region, and the land and its inhabitants had never been fully able to break free from that particular momentum. The area was only just attempting it when I was in my childhood years—the 1960s.

My Aunt Vernelle lived her entire life (up until present day) just outside of town in an area known as Trinity Mountain. The home she made with her husband and son was modest and well-kept, but without most of the amenities now found in the suburban sprawl which passes for neighborhoods nowadays. The house did have electricity and indoor plumbing, but that was about it. When it came to everything else, Aunt Vernelle might as well have been in the last century. While the rest of the world had caught up to grocery stores and the beginnings of strip malls, the family Aunt Vernelle belonged to did things the old-fashioned way.

I remember once visiting her on a bright blue-and-white summer day when I was about ten years old. This involved an extensive drive into the countryside. That had to be around 1964. After turning off the highway and onto a dirt road barely wide enough for one car, we arrived at the unassuming home of Aunt Vernelle and Uncle Bud. It was a white clapboard structure badly in need of a touch-up job. Two large gnarled oaks planted themselves on each side of the dirt path that led to the front door, and all around the house, before the land began to go wild again, were planted flowers of every shape and size. There wasn't another house near it for miles.

Before the car had come to a complete stop that day, I opened the door and ran into the house well ahead of my mother. I found Nelle in the kitchen, seated behind an odd wooden object with a long handle sticking upright out of it. Immediately I ran up to her, but she didn't stop what she was doing.

"Come here and give me a peck on the cheek," she said, never once stopping the repetitive motion she was engaged in. I did as I was told and then stepped back.

She could tell by the look on my face that I was wondering what she was up to as I stood before the tapering cylinder of wood gripped between the faded cotton knees of her dress.

"She's making butter," I heard my mother answer in reference to my puzzled expression as she entered the back door to the kitchen, bearing several bolts of cloth she had bought on the way to our visit. We had stopped at a small general store and my mother had picked up odds and ends while I tried to decide which bottled Co-Cola was the coldest in the enormous ice chest that stood on the sagging front porch of the store.

"Why doesn't she just buy it like everyone else?" I asked in response to the butter comment. Then I turned to my aunt. "Why don't you just buy it like everyone else?" I repeated, as though my aunt might not have heard me.

"Now there ain't no need to spend good money on something you can make yourself," she answered. Momentarily that seemed to satisfy me, and it was just one incident, this churning of butter, but it told me volumes about Vernelle and her family.

The bolts of cloth that my mother had brought her sister were yet another piece to the puzzle, but at the time I was too preoccupied with other things to figure it out. You see, my aunt made not only her own clothes, but those of her husband and children, with the exception of a few pairs of overalls for the men in the family and the occasional hat and gloves she wore while attending church.

"That gingham'll make a nice day dress," said Nelle to my mother who was busy sorting through some containers of pickles and preserves that had just recently been put up.

"Nelle, I'll buy six of these jars of sweet pickles if you'll sell them to me," my mother said as she turned one of the shimmering jars in the light. The afternoon sun sliced through the dusty window over the sink, sank itself deep into the floating liquid and cucumbers, and reflected pieces of green light about the kitchen. Store-bought food coloring had been added for the desired effect.

"Shsssss. Ain't goin' to sell them. Just take you six. You brought me this bolt of cloth anyway," said my aunt. My mother moved six of the jars over to one side and then began eyeing the preserves. "And pick you out three or four of *them* too," Nelle said, seeing my mother's interest. During this entire conversation, my aunt never once missed a beat at the churn. I was intrigued by my mother's interest in the jars of brightly colored fruits and vegetables. We usually shopped at the Piggly-Wiggly where everything was sanitized and new. These jars, the churn, and some of the things I would later stumble on, would give me new insight into how not only some of my relatives lived, but how my mother had grown up. She and Nelle had been the only children of a white sharecropper family in northern Alabama during the depression. While my mother had moved onward and upward to the big city of Sheffield, Alabama, Aunt Vernelle had stayed behind, not wanting to leave the only place she had ever known. And while she had eventually married my Uncle Bud and they had moved into this house, she was never very far away from home since their property sat up against the old worn-out fields that my grandfather used to plow in the thirties. Even the broken-down house that my grandparents had lived in was still visible across fields of cotton and indefatigable kudzu.

"Nelle," my mother continued, "when does Bud get back from hunting?

"Shoot. He's done been back already. Look there in the sink." While Nelle was addressing my mother, I followed suit and walked over to the ancient oversized receptacle on cast-iron legs. My mother saw my eyes widen as I peered over the edge.

"They're space men," I said, real fear rising in my voice. Both women in the kitchen laughed and then my mother explained.

"They're rabbits and squirrels. They've just had the skin stripped off so they're all pink and smooth." I felt as though I was going to be sick so I made a quick exit out the screen door and onto the cool back porch. I wasn't one for the killing of animals, but I knew that Aunt Nelle and Uncle Bud weren't well off and that my uncle hunted for food and not for sport. While they might have been able to buy more store-bought food than they did, hunting and frugality were in the Dadefyfe's blood. It was a habit that was hard to break.

I sat down among the large rusted coffee cans containing bits of vines and mint plants, staring off into the pasture in back of the house. Two cows lazily grazed several yards in the distance and a horse's tail shooed flies away, its small form barely visible as it was almost a half-mile from the porch, near a large, leaning barn which was surrounded by sycamore and hickory trees.

"Reckon Bud'll mind if I take him down to the barn?" I heard my mother ask Nelle. Only an outline of her was visible through the screen door. "I want him to milk a cow and get eggs out of the hen house. He needs to know what it's like growing up in the country."

I always found it amusing how my mother's speech changed once she came in contact with her relatives or this geographical part of the county. She seemed to regress in some way—nothing bad, just different. It was her language that was the most telling. Whereas it had once been proper and full, it was now somewhat twangy and peppered with "ain'ts" and "reckons."

"And I want him out there picking cotton, too. Lord, do you remember the times we had to get out in that field, bent over and picking that stuff with those bolls scratching up our hands? I'll never forget the time that neighbor girl, Het, wasn't that her name, picked up one of them grasshoppers by mistake and let out a yell that could be heard all the way over to Colbert County." Both my mother and Aunt Nelle laughed at this, but all I could do was try to imagine my mother picking cotton. I tried to visualize her in the field, but it was a stretch as she now dressed up most of the time and worked in a bank in Sheffield. I knew that my mother and her sister had grown up on a farm, but I had always envisioned them just having to throw some hay to the farm animals and occasionally pick some overgrown cucumber. This picking cotton sounded serious.

Then it hit me. She was talking about having *me* milk the cow, gather eggs, and pick cotton. What was she thinking? I decided to jump off the porch and see what I could find to amuse myself in the hope that, if she didn't forget this idea, at least when it came time to perform the duties, I would be nowhere in sight. I knew she meant well, but the country life just wasn't for me. I wanted to be back home in Sheffield where the most exotic thing we ate was spaghetti and meatballs. I rambled across the backyard and was halfway through a thick patch of elephant ears at the side of the house when I parted two enormous leaves and found myself staring down the barrel of a large silver gun.

"Move once and you're dead," a voice said from behind one of the iridescent leaves which had begun to show signs of brown around its border—a result of the intense north Alabama summer air. I swallowed hard and stood my ground.

"Clement, get me that rope," the voice ordered to a rustling movement on the other side of a rather motley forsythia bush. "Now tie him up. We can't have his kind running loose in these parts," continued the individual who now made his appearance through the leaves, wearing a red straw cowboy hat, red chaps, and a pair of overly pointed red cowboy boots. The gun was still aimed directly at my head and its owner squinted unmercifully at me. A long thin piece of Johnson grass dangled smartly from the corner of his mouth.

"Hey Jules," I said, recognizing my cousin who was several years older than me. About this time, Clement, the boy who lived down the road from my Aunt Vernelle and her family, appeared with the rope and proceeded to tie my arms to my body as he circled me in a slow methodical fashion. Clement was a good three years older than Jules, but he sure didn't act it. People said he wasn't quite right in the head, but it didn't seem to matter to Jules as Clement was the only playmate he had within five miles. The neighbor boy was big for his age and could have easily passed for a high school senior. It was said he wouldn't make it past the ninth grade.

"What are y'all playing, Jules?" I asked as I stood completely still, allowing Clement to circle me. He still had what appeared to be several dozen feet of rope left and was already out of breath.

"You shut up," said Jules. "We know you was responsible for the robbery of the stagecoach last night, so there's no use in lyin'." By this time Clement had tired of his circling and was weaving his way over to a pile of split logs. "Deputies ain't no use nowadays," said Jules, casting a glance over at Clem, and relegated his toy gun to his holster as he walked bowlegged over to where the large boy was now sitting, holding his head.

"Can't help it," whined Clement, "I feel sick."

"You brought too much durn rope, Clement. I done told you to get the small rope outa my daddy's fishing boat but you wouldn't listen."

"I'm going home," said Clement, dropping his toy gun belt and metal star badge. He staggered over to the barbed-wire fence that separated the neighbor's property from that of my Uncle Bud and Aunt Vernelle.

"Looks like it's just you and me," said Jules, and proceeded to unwind the rope while standing in one spot. Jules was several inches taller than me, so all he had to do was swing his arm around my head and the rope unfurled like some giant backwards lasso, expanding in circumference until it was touching the ground. "Here. Strap these on," he said, and handed me the gun belt. I pinned the metal star onto my shirt. Then he looked me over, up and down. "Naw. Something ain't right. What you needs is a horse."

"I'm not getting on any horse," I said, looking down and rolling my eyes up at him.

"Not a real horse. Come on. I got an idea." Then he stopped. "How tall you, boy?" He again eyed me up and down. Then he was off to the other side of the house. I watched as he rolled two large stones in my direction, letting them fall about a foot and a half apart.

"Here now. You stand here, on these rocks," he said, and as soon as I had done so and he was secure in the knowledge that I wasn't going anywhere, he turned and ran off in the direction of the pen where his father kept the hunting dogs. I stayed where he had told me to, but looked over my shoulder to see him emerge through the tall dry brown grass. Just after him, the slender stalks parted to reveal one of his father's dogs.

"This here's Crook. My daddy just took him out this morning to hunt so he won't be using him no more today," he said and led the dog toward me.

"What are you doing?" I started to ask, but before I could finish, Jules had led the dog directly between my legs and I was now straddling the creature who looked up at me with a silly slobbering grin.

"Go ahead," said Jules, "sit down on him."

"I can't sit down on him. He's a dog," I said.

"He can take it. He's a big guy and you're a small guy. You're not too heavy. If you was a couple years older like me you couldn't do it, but you're little. Go ahead."

So as easily as I could I lowered my weight onto Crook. But no sooner had I sat down than he bolted straight toward the barbed-wire fence. I hung on like a bronco rider and was just about to put my arms around his neck when he suddenly stopped with his head down and one paw in front, throwing me under the first line of barbed wire. A rather motley group of irises cushioned my fall.

"Them's momma's flowers. She'll raise living hell if she finds out you mashed 'em," said Jules.

"What was that?" I asked, getting up and dusting off my pride and the seat of my pants, completely ignoring his reference to the sad-looking plants.

"Crook's a pointer. He seen something in them weeds, maybe a rabbit, maybe a quail, and he pointed. That's what he does. He's a German shorthaired pointer. Old man Gillespie who lives down the road wanted to get rid of him and Daddy took him. Daddy says he's the best bird dog in the area.

"Why's he called 'Crook?' " I asked, trying to postpone getting back atop the dog.

" 'Cause he steals things," said Jules with great annoyance, as if I should have known this bit of information.

"What kinda things?" I asked. It was becoming obvious even to Crook that I was attempting to get out of another mounting.

"Hell, he done stole my best baseball glove last summer and chewed the durn thing clean up. Before that it was a decoy duck of my daddy, and then it was one of mamma's flour sack towels off-un the clothesline out back," continued Jules.

Crook just stood there, his head turning from Jules to me, looking far too happy for any dog. After a moment, he let out a good-natured "Woof."

"Then maybe I shouldn't be riding him," I said, thinking that any dog that was a kleptomaniac might have other emotional problems.

"I done told you that you ain't gonna hurt him. Besides, when I was littler than I am now I rode him. Now git back on and lets git started."

I climbed back onto Crook, this time without the aid of the two rocks, and gripped his sides with my legs. My feet just barely skimmed the ground. He didn't seem to mind, and this time he moved more slowly as Jules had him by a worn brown leather leash.

"You come on now and I'm a gonna take you into the sheriff's office," said Jules as he led us through a patch of weeds and back into the yard between the house and the pasture.

Fortunately, after an hour or so, Jules tired of his imaginary game and withdrew into the house to see when supper would be ready. I stayed on the back porch trying to figure out how many shapes I could make out of the clouds as the day began to wind down. After a while Crook came over and put his head in my lap with his big eyes looking up at me. The dog was as good-natured as they come. I could have slung him over my shoulder and carried him like a sack of potatoes and he wouldn't have minded a bit, but looking deep within his eyes was another story. There wasn't anything bad there; nothing to tell you that he might someday hurt you. Quite the contrary, he was the most loving dog in the whole world. But it was almost as if he'd seen things past and present and wanted to share them with you, and knowing that he lacked speech and that you probably wouldn't believe him anyway, he simply resigned himself to hoping that you'd someday figure them out. That was the look. It wasn't exactly pity, but rather a look that said he knew things were going to happen and he only wished he could stay around to be of comfort. Almost like he'd done the whole thing—life—before.

I looked at his deep brown eyes and was peering into them, trying to see my reflection, when suddenly Crook cut to the pasture and flew off my lap as if someone had stuck a lit match to his private parts.

"Crook! Heeeah, heeeah!" It was Bud, my uncle, Vernelle's husband, coming in from the woods in back of the pasture. Crook flew to his side and was rewarded with a rough pat from the man's thick, weathered hands. "Good boy, good boy," muttered the old man as he roughed the liver-colored fur on Crook's back. Then he took the dog by the head and flopped his ears from side to side.

Bud wasn't much more than a pair of faded blue overalls and green Wellington waders, with what was left of a once-vibrant young man stuffed inside. At one time considered the handsomest man in three counties, Bud was now thin and looking more than his fifty-some-odd years. He had worked hard all his life and even though he had made enough money to live more comfortably than he and Vernelle did, he was frugal, being a person of Scottish descent, and insisted on keeping the family spending to a minimum. Hence the hunting for squirrel and rabbit when ground beef could just have easily been bought at McCullough's General Store on the south side of Moulton. Bud and Vernelle Dadefyfe were poor—they just weren't *that* poor.

"You'n Crook been keepin' each other company?" he shouted at me as he mounted the steps with his heavy boots, and gave the top of my head the same treatment as he had given Crook, sans the ear flopping. Uncle Bud was slightly deaf.

"Yes, sir," I said loudly and watched the saggy rear end of his overalls disappear behind the rusted screen door. Crook's gaze followed the man inside, but his body remained behind with me, and after a few seconds he turned his attention in my direction, rewarding my back-porch tenacity with a wet sandpaper tongue which seemed to go a good three inches inside my right ear. I swung my arm around his neck and buried my nose in his fur. It smelled of dirt and pheasant blood and all things connected with the earth.

"Jack, you and Jules go get washed up for supper," my Aunt Vernelle yelled to the air in the kitchen. From the back of the house I could hear a commotion as Jules was now trying to hog-tie some inanimate object in his bedroom. I could hear him because it was summer and the windows were open. A giant square fan drew the hot Alabama air from the house and pushed it into the yard. When its mechanism was put on reverse it often sucked in unsuspecting beetles and wasps, sending them hurtling into a bureau mirror directly across from the apparatus.

"And now, the greatest rodeo rider of them all . . . and the crowd goes wild," Jules mimicked to no one in particular. Occasionally he would move too close to the fan and the heavy oscillating blades would throw his voice, dream-like and wavy, toward the pasture in back of the house.

Crook sauntered over to the wooden steps and descended, turning to look up at me. I sat still for a moment, just watching him. Then he nosed at something under the house, looked back up at me, and nosed again, as if trying to tell me to follow. I got up to have a look.

When I was at the bottom of the steps, Crook crawled into an opening just beside one of the brick columns holding up the structure. My eyes tried to track him into the cool, earthy darkness, but I couldn't formulate anything. Then he turned around while under the house, and picking up something in his mouth, showed me what was left of a catcher's mitt—Jules's catcher's mitt. When he returned the object to its resting place, I bent down further, intent on inspecting what he was up to. If I tilted my head just so and looked up under the edifice, I could make out the space where Crook was now comfortably resting. A gap in the flooring the size of a giant splinter allowed just enough light to penetrate the darkness and make visible not only the dog, but his bounty of objects that he so coveted. Just as Jules had said, there was a flour sack towel and even the body of a decoy duck, its head neatly chewed off. There were other objects too—small trophies that Crook had gleaned from the Dadefyfe family and stowed onto his soft pine-needle bed—a chewed-up rubber ball, the bone from a pot roast, a now-defunct bedroom shoe.

Satisfied that we had shared a moment, Crook came out from under the house and slowly began to wonder through the backyard and toward the pasture, loping about in almost circles. And as the cool of the evening began to descend on the hot dry land of Alabama, I mounted the steps to the back porch, opened the squeaky screen door, and made my way into the kitchen.

"And the crowd goes wiiiiiiilllllldddd . . ." sang Jules into the vibrating fan.

Two

"You didn't tell me we were staying for supper," I said, looking up at my mother who was standing over the sink, attempting to wrench a rabbit's leg free from the rest of the poor bunny. The animal's fur lay forlornly to one side on some brown paper bags.

"We're just staying one night," she said, looking down at me. "I grew up in the country and I want you to get to know the things I knew as a child. Tomorrow you're going to pick cotton and milk the cows."

"You've got to be kidding me, right?" I said, looking at her with my most horrified stare. Distracted at that moment, she jerked her arm back and the rabbit's leg tore free from the rest of its body, accidentally sending a splatter of blood directly across my face.

I howled and ran out the back door once again, attracting the attention of Crook who came running through the pasture toward me, eager to see what anxiety I had now provoked. My knees buckled and I found myself sitting on top of one of my aunt's tin washtubs. By this time Crook had found me, and his tongue licked the squirrel's blood from my face. After a moment or two, my mother appeared at the screen door with hands on hips, looking down at me. She didn't say anything at first, and I just stared back at her, the whole time with Crook still cleaning my face and arms.

"It's just a little blood, Jack. Don't be such a sissy. At least Crook doesn't seem to mind," she said, and then disappeared back into the kitchen with a little laugh.

Dinner was late afternoon/early evening, just after the sun had gone down. The participants included my aunt and uncle, my mother, myself, and Jules who was now wearing another cowboy outfit, exactly like the one he had worn previously, only in the color blue: blue hat, blue chaps, blue overly-pointed cowboy boots.

"Is the blue one only for after-five dining?" I asked, genuinely curious, but my mother's glance put an end to the questioning.

"Ain't you going to eat your dinner?" Nelle asked me after a while, noticing my untouched squirrel, mashed potatoes, and green beans. The mashed potatoes I could possibly handle, but I had seen a pig's snout floating in the green beans when they were on the stove—on purpose no less—and I was considering eating the squirrel if at some point I was made to choose.

"I'm really not very hungry," I said and proceeded to form a path in the mashed potatoes, complete with tire gullies like the ones I had seen on some of the back roads after a good rain. The fork proved beneficial for this task. While I could certainly appreciate certain aspects of country living, some of the food I could have done without. About the most exotic thing my mother made was turnip greens and I considered these a stretch for someone at the age of ten. Still, there were mounds of fresh tomatoes, butter peas, onions, and corn—all from the garden in back of the house. I did have to admit that they tasted better than anything store-bought.

The supper hour in the country can be inordinately long, and this one was no exception. The merits of tractor-pulled plows and the electrified hen house that Old Man Jacobs had just installed being exhausted, it was time for dessert. Aunt Nelle had made a Lane cake, and since I couldn't immediately identify any animal parts that I knew of sticking out of it, I ate most of it.

After dinner the grownups went into the "parlor" (it was actually the living room *and* den, but was called by this name because it had been so christened for the past hundred years) to talk, and Jules and I went into his bedroom. At least that's what we told them. Once in the back, we removed the fan from Jules's bedroom window and lowered ourselves down the side of the house and onto the cool wet green grass. In the process, a long forsythia branch caught me in the eye and I feel to my knees.

"Come on. Get up. We don't have much time," said Jules and pulled me to my feet. He looked at my eye in the dark, pretending to be able to see. "It looks okay. Ain't nothing wrong with it. Just a scratch. You'll be all right."

We crossed under the barbed wire fence and were about halfway through the pasture when he took my arm, physically ordering me to stop without speaking. There in the early evening were a group of cows, perfectly still, their rotund posteriors perfectly silhouetted against a blue-black sky full of stars.

"Stand here just a minute," he whispered in my ear. I stood in the moonlit pasture and breathed in the crisp smell of evening and hay. It wasn't long before I spotted a shape moving toward us, gingerly side-stepping the many "cow patties" that littered the pasture. In no time the figure was beside us.

"What took you so long, Clement?" admonished Jules with a perturbed look that I could see even in the moonlight.

"I was busy with somethin'," said Clement and looked slightly embarrassed.

"Well, what was you busy with?" prodded Jules.

"Just shut up, will ya?" responded Clem, and his harsh tone seemed to placate Jules and put an end to the questioning. Even I could figure out what the big secret was, and I was truly astonished that Jules, for all his experience around farm animals and nature, couldn't grasp the situation.

"Okay, here's the plan," said Jules. Clem and I automatically huddled around like we were athletes on a football field receiving instructions on a play. "First, I'm gonna go over to the far side of that cow and spread them bales of hay down. Daddy'd kill us all if we injured one of his milk cows. Second, I'm gonna come back here. When I say go, all three of us'll run toward her. Now we got to make sure we git to her the same time so as to put all our weight into her. Clem, you git on the left and I'll git on the right. That way Jack can be in the middle since he's the smallest. Everybody got it?"

We nodded agreement and Jules started off in the direction of the unsuspecting bovine. "What's going to happen?" I asked Clem. I figured that he might actually tell me, and if he thought I was dumb by asking, at least I would only have an overgrown neighbor thinking I was stupid and not my cousin. Besides, if Clem made a big deal out of it, I could always say he was lying. Everyone knew he had some screws loose.

"We're gonna tip that cow," said Clem, as matter-of-factly as if you'd said, "That'll be forty-nine ninety-five."

It was all new to me, but I figured that it had to be more fun than eating squirrel and so I decided to go along with the thing. I tried to imagine giving the cow a crisp five-dollar bill for performing some function such as waiting on our table while we sat at the "Why Not Café?" in downtown Moulton. "Would you all like to see a dessert menu, Hon?" I imagined her asking, bored with the same routine day after day, chewing her cud while she waited for our answer. But my reverie was cut short. In a few moments Jules returned out of breath.

"Okay. She's still asleep so we can git goin'," he said.

"Asleep?" I asked

"You don't think we'd be tippin' no cow that was wide awake, do you?" Jules asked with his hands on his hips. His blue cowboy outfit shone almost iridescent in the moonlight and he looked remarkably authoritative and in control.

"I guess not," I said, ashamed at not having figured out this line of thought myself.

"Now let's start running and when we git close, I'll count three and we have to arrive at her at the same time so's she'll fall over."

All three of us started to run, and just as we were picking up speed and nearing the unsuspecting animal, I slipped in what was probably the largest pile of cow excrement known to farmkind, and landed facedown in the pasture. I looked up just in time to see the four-legged animal fall with a thud onto the hay that Jules had thoughtfully spread out beforehand. Before the old girl even hit the ground, Jules and Clem were over the fence and looking on from a safe position.

I got up and tried to brush off what I could of the pasture that had attached itself to my blue jeans, and was about to walk in their direction when I felt an eerie presence near me. I thought that maybe dairy humor just wasn't my style, and that I was worrying needlessly, but the feeling didn't go away and I began to get anxious.

At first I just felt its breath—great bursts of saliva-soaked air shooting out of its nostrils—and for a moment my mind tried to make sense of the new sensation. The realization that the animal in back of me was a cow was only amplified by the recognition that it *wasn't*. Now I knew that the horse was in the barn, so I was left with only one choice. Before I had a chance to react, I heard Jules's voice being thrown in a stage whisper in my direction. "Just walk slowly toward us and whatever you do, don't ruuuuun," he said as gently as he could. I decided that I would follow his instructions, but before I did I turned my head to look at whatever it was behind me.

Even by the light of the moon I could make out its shape—the largest bull I had ever seen in my life. The unfortunate part was, at that exact moment, Jules finished his instructions to me. "Whatever you dooooooo, don't Loooooook at the buuuuull."

To make matters worse, because of the time lapse between the tipped cow and my discovery of her husband, the first creature had managed to regain her footing, and was none too pleased. For those that think I was brave in my long peregrination toward Jules and Clem, let me assure you—I didn't have much of a choice. I certainly wasn't going to stand in the pasture for the rest of my life and I was too scared to run, so I did the next best thing, which fortunately, was the correct move. I walked slowly toward the nearest fence, pretending I was supposed to be there at that time of night. It paid off, because I escaped unscathed. But I was totally unnerved as the bull had followed me with its huge black nose stuck *into* my rear end, prodding me out of his territory. Whenever he thought that I was slacking off in my attempt to leave the pasture, his enormous head would root upward and a blast from his nostrils would soak the seat of my pants.

When I arrived at Jules and Clem, they were doubled over with silent laughter, rolling in the manure-free grass on the bull-free side of the fence. I just stood there, furious.

"Well, what did you want us to do?" asked Jules when he had calmed down, "Go in there and get you? Hell, that bull's about the meanest thing in the whole county. We weren't sure you'd git out alive."

"I slipped in a cow patty," I said, looking down at my soiled pants.

"Looks to me like you slipped in the whole durn pasture," said Clement, and he and Jules started to laugh again. It was one thing to be laughed at by Jules, but another entirely to be laughed at by an overgrown, not-quite-right-in-the-head, too-friendly-with-his-right-hand-adolescent.

By this time I had had enough and began to make my way back to the house in a huff. I was almost to the back door when Jules caught up with me and spun me around. "You can't go in that way. If they find out we were out here tippin' the cows we'll get the switch for sure," he said. "Come on. We've got to crawl back in the window," and he pulled me toward the side of the house.

"I'll make a cup with my hand like this, see," he said, bending over and linking his fingers together. "Then you step up in it and hoist yourself up to the sill. Once you get in you can pull me up. Take them shoes off first." I followed the directions and for some reason the plan worked perfectly. Once in his bedroom we could hear the grownups as their conversation began to wind down. We had both shed our clothes and were now on Jules's bed. The springs beneath the mattress squeaked and the blankets smelled musty, like they had been outside on the ground, but the overly soft mattress rose up and engulfed us both. We lay there silently, waiting for the rest of the house to go to sleep.

After a few minutes, a sliver of light came into the room from the cracked bedroom door. It was my mother. She came over to my side of the bed and stroked my hair.

"You awake?" she asked

"No'm," I said, trying to make my eyelids look heavy.

"Well, you get some rest. Tomorrow you've got a busy day. Aunt Vernelle is going to get you up at five o'clock so you can milk the cows," she said.

I don't remember when it was that I fell asleep, but I do know it was well after Jules had dozed off. I lay there for the longest time, wondering how I always seemed to get myself into these messes.

Three

There's something about getting out of a warm bed on a cold morning that is particularly obscene. It's just not natural. Especially at five o'clock. I'm sure there is some "farm" rationale for rising at this early hour, but as a city boy, or at least a suburban one, the plan escaped me. My Aunt Nelle arrived in Jules's bedroom with a clean pair of overalls for me and some work boots that just happened to fit.

Lucky me.

"These were Jules's a few years ago," she said as she laid them on the chair next to where I was still warmly covered. "Now you boys get up. There's plenty for you to do today, and Jack, your mother wants you to get her some eggs out of the hen house."

Jules saw the look on my face and decided to offer me some words of comfort. "Ain't nothin' to it," he said, the handmade quilt still firmly pulled up to his chin. "I just thank God it's one day I don't have to do it. You ought to come visit more often. Then maybe I'd git out of some of the chores more usual like."

I knew there was no use saying anything. My mother had insisted that I learn the ways of the country, so in the event that I ever went to live in some big city I would have a proper perspective on things. I would be able to see the good and the bad in both and make my decisions more readily. At least that's what I told myself.

"Is it hard?" I asked Jules as I reluctantly got out of bed and reached for the overalls. They appeared to be almost starched and were the slightest bit too short. I stood there trying to imagine that they fit.

"Naw. It's real easy once you git the hang of it. " 'Sides, Momma is gonna show you how to milk the cow. All you gots to do to git the eggs is to shoo the chickens off the nest first." He paused for dramatic effect. "And hope there ain't no snakes hanging around waiting for a free meal."

"Snakes?"

"Well, we do git them from time to time."

I finished with my dressing and headed out to the kitchen to see about breakfast.

"No, now. There ain't no breakfast until after the chores is done," said Nelle, and she knelt down to my level. "My, don't you look just like Jules a few years ago. You come on now, out here to the barn with me and we're gonna milk that old cow." She took my hand and led me out across the backyard. I noticed how her simple cotton dress clung to her. It was clean and smelled faintly of starch and lilac water. Her skin was smooth and just beginning to show signs of aging—you know, when things begin to soften and sag slightly. It was nothing unattractive, but rather an appearance that tells you the person has been through a lot—that they've *lived.*

When we were halfway to the barn, Crook appeared beside us, wagging his tail. "Looks like old Crook's gonna' help us with them chores today," said Nelle.

I was impressed. Both Crook and Nelle were able to side-step every cow patty with remarkable expertise, almost as if they had radar. They never once looked down, yet never made a mistake. I, on the other hand, could barely walk without at least hitting the side of one of these hardened piles of cow feces, and I was looking down the entire time in an effort to improve my chances.

Nelle creaked open the weathered barn door and immediately we were greeted by moos from the cows and the squabble of chickens. A solitary chicken dropped squawking from one of the rafters, and I jumped a good three feet into the air. In one of the stalls a horse whinnied and threw his head back. Through it all my aunt led me calmly down the open center of the barn and toward a stall where the cows had been penned.

"Were these cows here all night?" I asked as we approached a familiar brown-and white-spotted one.

"Lord, no. They was out in the pasture last night. I just rounded them up this morning."

My heart sank. While I hadn't actually pushed any cows over, I had been seen in the pasture by both Mr. and Mrs. Bovine and I was sure they had all conferred with each other over a breakfast of grass and dandelions, and were all plotting my demise.

"Now you sit here on this here stool," said my aunt, "and just let me get a bucket to put the milk in." While she went into another part of the barn I tried to act nonchalant. I hoped that the cow didn't recognize me, and even if it did, if I acted casual, that it would figure I wasn't worth the trouble of intimidating.

I was wrong.

My aunt had not been gone more than a full minute when the beast I was sitting under turned its enormous head, and out of the moist lower end of its face emitted the loudest "moooo" I had ever heard. For anyone who has not heard a cow "moo" up close, there is nothing pastoral about it. These things are *loud.*

I could see Bessie's lungs fill up and then her stout body contract as she forced the air from all eight of her stomachs, all the way out through her cow lips. I was up off the stool in no time, looking for the nearest escape route.

"She didn't kick, did she?" my aunt asked as she set the pail down underneath the cow. She had returned just after Bessie's earth-shattering "moooo."

"Kick? She kicks too?" I asked.

"Sometimes. You have to be careful of the back end."

I thought to myself how the front end wasn't that friendly either, but didn't say anything.

"Now this isn't that hard," began my aunt. "You just take one of these udders between these fingers like this and pull down slightly and squeeze."

"You're kidding me, right?" I said, with a totally serious tone, just the way I had questioned my mother the day before when confronted with the possibility of eating a cute small furry animal that I associated with acorns and construction paper leaves.

"Oh, my! You are such a precious child," she said and hugged me. "Now you sit here and try it." Aunt Vernelle was a lot of things, but totally perceptive wasn't one of them, and this probably worked to my advantage. That, plus the fact that she didn't have a malicious bone in her body.

I sat down and reached for the underside of the cow, but something stopped me. Perhaps it was the thought of touching a thing as private as a cow's under parts, or perhaps it was my guilt from the night before when poor Bessie had been unsuspectingly toppled over like some Marxist leader's statue during the fall of Communism. Whatever the reason, I just couldn't do it.

"Now don't be scared of her," my aunt said. "She's just as gentle as she can be and she's used to this." Then she squatted next to me and took my hand in hers. "Look, just let your hand go limp and put it in mine. I'll do it for you so you can feel what it's like."

Somehow, with Aunt Nelle's hand around mine the whole experience wasn't so scary, and the first time the raw milk squirted out with an unnatural force from the rubbery udder, I felt almost joyful. I laughed out loud and the cow let out another "moo," though this time less frightening. Crook—now settled in the corner with what appeared to be a large bone—barked his approval and I begged to be allowed to try the whole thing by myself. When the pail was half full and the cow appeared to be drying out, I felt a sadness at having the task come to an end. Crook sauntered over to me, wagging his tail, and began licking the overly-sweet milk from my hands. It seemed this dog would lick anything, but I couldn't be critical—I had never felt such love for an animal and it seemed that it was being constantly returned.

"All we have to do is get us about a dozen eggs and we'll be ready to go have breakfast," said Nelle, and with that she took the pail from me and we headed into the section of the barn the chickens roosted in.

"Shooo, shoo, shoo," she said, wiping her hand into the air several times, and the squawking hens scattered in every direction. "There. Here are some nice ones," she said, holding up several of the eggs to the light.

"How come they're brown and not white?" I asked as she put two of the eggs into the basket.

"Eggs is supposed to be brown. Only them that you get from the grocery store is white. These are the real thing. Just from the chicken. Here, you take this basket and be careful not to break any."

I took the basket and proceeded to gather the eggs. I had about six and felt myself a pro when suddenly one of the hens came flapping at my head. Again, where barnyard life is concerned, the creatures rarely resemble the docile stereotypes of children's books and cartoons. Chickens have always appeared to be quite small to me (having only seen them when they are roasted and presented on the kitchen table for Sunday dinner), but this thing was enormous. At least it seemed that way with its wingspan and its loud cawing.

"What's it want?" I yelled to my aunt as I tried to protect myself with my arm.

"You get on out of here! Shoo, shooo!" screamed my aunt at the chicken and the thing sulked off into a corner, seeming to mutter to itself. "She's the nastiest old hen. I keep thinking that we'll have her one day for dinner, but she's the best producer we've got. Ain't that the way it always goes? The one who gives you the majority of trouble is usually the one that gives you the most." Then she looked into my basket. "Let's just get a few more and then we can go have breakfast."

Four

Breakfast was thankfully less eventful than dinner the night before. I had seen eggs before they were cooked, and while the ones I was used to were white, I could forgive this small difference. Besides, I was starving from not having eaten much last night. After we had finished, my aunt looked at me and asked, "Are you ready to go pick some cotton?"

"No," I responded, without malice. I thought that the barn experiences were enough to fill up my day and I would rather have been out back in the elephant ears, playing cowboys and macramé salesman than stooped over in some hot field where the visuals were even less appealing. She had a funny look on her face, so I revised my answer. "No, ma'am, thank you though," I said, hoping to soften my first response.

It wasn't anything that she said at that point—my Aunt Vernelle—but rather the extreme negative energy that I felt coming from one corner of the room. I turned to see my mother with her hands on her hips and a frown forming on her face. Then I turned back to my aunt. "I'd love to see what it's like to pick cotton," I said, forcing a smile.

"We'll all go," said my mother, after dusting the flour off of her hands. She was attempting to make a pie crust the way

Vernelle had demonstrated earlier that day, but wasn't able to quite get the hang of it. Well, at least that was a relief. I had envisioned myself the solitary figure in the middle of some field with only a couple of blow flies and a rattlesnake to keep me company.

Before too long we were making our way around the side of the cow pasture and down the dirt road that led to several acres of now-ready cotton. "Why isn't Jules coming with us?" I asked, seeing that only my aunt and mother were making the trip.

"Jules has got other work to do," said my aunt, handing me a large flour sack.

"What's this for?"

"That's to put the cotton in. You've got to fill that up before we can go home," said Nelle. About this time Crook came bounding out of a patch of high grass and swung onto the road, falling in step behind the three of us.

"Old Crook sure does love you," said my aunt, looking down at the dog. He responded by lolling his tongue out to one side and giving an airy "woof" in her direction.

"Don't care much for hunting dogs," said my mother. "How many you reckon Bud's got now?"

"Shoot. He's got near forty or so, but ain't none of them as good as Crook. Them German pointers has got the best disposition if you ask me," answered my aunt.

No sooner had Nelle finished her last sentence than Crook bolted a few feet to the left of us, hung his head low, and pointed. "See there," said Nelle, "he's done found him either a rabbit or some quail. Run on over there and flush it out, Jack."

I ran up behind Crook and directly up to the side of the road where he was pointing. Four mourning doves took flight and squeaked into the intense blue sky.

"Now if Bud was here, he would have shot them birds and you'd be eating them for dinner," said my aunt. I couldn't help but feel grateful that Bud wasn't here, for I didn't think I could go without eating another meal. My mother may have grown up in the country, eating what food came from the land, but I was strictly a hamburger and fries kind of person.

Not long after the four doves took to the sky, we turned down a smaller dirt road and made our way through a fence of branches and barbed wire. Deep tire tracks cut through the thick red Alabama mud and the earth seemed to peel back from them like some sort of ornate clay sculpture, frozen in time until the next hard rain. In the thick grasses surrounding the fields, insects carried on a festival of song, and high above us a lone hawk momentarily suspended itself before swooping into a thicket of cottonwood trees.

"Now, Jack, you and Crook can start on this row and your momma and I'll start on the other side. First let me show you how you do it," said Nelle, bending down to the nearest cotton boll. "Come on down here so you can see, Jack," she continued. My mother shook her head. "Lord, it's been years since I've done this, Nelle. I remember when we were kids and Momma and Daddy'd get the switch after us if we came back with only half a sack."

My aunt looked up at my mother as her fingers dug into the fibrous white cotton that had burst open from within the outer hard shell. Then she wrenched free the coveted bloom and held it up for me to see. "Now this here cotton has got seeds in it. When we get back to the house I'll show you how we get the seeds out. There's something called a cotton comb that'll separate them from the cotton. Here now, you try just like I done."

I reached down into one of the hard shells that had burst open and pulled the clean white froth from its resting place. I could feel the somewhat slimy seeds as they nestled inside their protective white covering. I pulled off the remaining pieces of hard boll and placed the insides into my bag. It didn't amount to much sitting in the bottom of the flour sack and I couldn't imagine my mother and her sister having to fill one of these or get switched. "That's right. Now just keep going until you get to the end of the row and then start back on the next one."

I began the assigned task, thinking that at least I didn't have to touch any private parts of some barnyard animal, and soon I felt myself a pro at removing the fluffy white insides of the bloom. For the most part Crook sat next to me, getting up every few feet or so to get a better view of my picking abilities.

Every so often he would trot along the rows and flush out some unsuspecting grasshopper and then return to my side. "Are you enjoying yourself?" I asked him. He didn't say anything, but again responded with lolling tongue and a jerk of his head upward. "Shame you can't help me with this row I've got to finish." He came forward and nuzzled his cold nose to my elbow.

After what seemed like a lifetime of gleaning the cotton from their natural casings, I surveyed how much damage I had done. It wasn't an uplifting sight. I thought I had picked every piece of cotton in Lawrence County only to find that I had moved a mere six feet. I still had a good two hundred yards to go, just on this one row, and there were probably several hundred rows in the field. I looked down into the flour sack and my depression grew even further. It's amazing how easily compressed cotton can become, and what I thought would amount to a sackfull as large as myself only came to something about the size of Crook's head.

I shaded my eyes with my hand and looked over at my Aunt Vernelle and my mother. "Hard work, ain't it?" said Nelle, and I nodded in agreement. I attempted to pick more of the plant, not wanting anyone to think me lazy, but this was backbreaking work and by the time I had assaulted three or four more bushes I had a new appreciation for what it must have been like for my mother and her sister. And if that was indeed the plan, then it was working marvelously.

"We better stop now. You look plum wore out," said Nelle. I looked down at Crook and he seemed to agree. We began our walk back down the road, but all at once the three of us stopped. Crook walked on ahead for a few feet, then circled and sat down in the middle of the thoroughfare. My mother and Nelle were looking at something in the distance, their hands held up over their eyes to shield the harsh sun that was now beating down on us.

"Lord have mercy," said my mother, again picking up on the native dialect, "I sure would love to see that old home place." There was silence for a moment, and then Nelle responded.

"Y'all want to go?" she asked, looking around at me, then my mother. But nothing was said. We simply started to walk in that direction, and after traversing another side road that was dirt and gullied, found ourselves before a dilapidated old house. The entire thing sagged in the middle, even the steep-pitched roof made of rusted tin, and the four posts in front looked as though they might give way any moment. Both rock chimneys had fallen to the ground, and there were gaping holes on each side of the structure. This was the house my mother and Nelle had been born in so many years ago, and it was the very location where they had been required to pick cotton and do the farm chores I was experiencing.

"It's been years since I've seen this old thing," my mother continued, and picked her way through the tall weeds surrounding the home. Nelle, Crook, and I followed after her, grateful for the path she had created through the tangled underbrush.

The front steps to the house were completely gone, so after my mother climbed up with the help of a rusting overturned bucket, she aided Nelle and me in our ascent. Crook just looked at us for a second, backed up, and then took a running leap onto the porch. All of us walked around on the precarious floorboards of the verandah for a while, testing what was left of the wood, hoping that we didn't find any weak spots. Then my mother tried the screen door. Within a minute we were standing inside the home my grandparents had lived in during the twenties and the Great Depression.

Immense hunks of faded wallpaper peeled themselves away from the plaster walls, and huge swaths of lathe and support beams were in plain view. While the floor didn't seem all that sturdy, it didn't appear to be rotten, and after determining this, all of us gained confidence and moved forward.

"Look at this old iron bed," my mother said, entering the first room on the left. "Many a time we both slept in that. And with the only heat being that old cast-iron stove in the kitchen." The bed was nothing more than a metal headboard and footboard with a series of ancient wires strung together for support of the mattress. About this time, we heard Crook make a commotion at the rear of the house. Following the noise, we found ourselves in the kitchen just in time to see a terrified rabbit leap through the space where a backdoor should have been, and off what was remaining of the porch. Crook didn't follow, but simply pointed, as if to say that even while on tour, on his day off, he could still prove his worth.

"Just one of them ole bunny rabbits," said my aunt, and I wondered how long it would be before Bud brought it home for dinner.

"Look at this," said my mother as she put her hand on the stove—the very one she had mentioned earlier. "Remember when Mamma used to cook on this thing? Times have really changed," she went on, and I thought to myself how they hadn't changed as much as she thought they had, at least not for some of the Dadefyfes.

Nelle bent down and opened the creaking door of the stove. Black soot fell onto the weathered boards of the kitchen floor. "I remember how I found out about where babies come from," she reminisced as she shut the door, wiping her hands on her simple cotton dress. "I come in one cold morning and there was two cats right here under this thing, stuck together like someone had glued them." She and my mother laughed, and then Nelle continued. "Lord, I tried to pry them things apart and they started howling like they was dying. Mamma came runnin' in and gave me the worst switchin' I ever got." By now, the two sisters were doubled over in laughter and even Crook joined in, barking his approval and turning circles. Then Nelle turned her attention to me. "We shouldn't be talkin' like this in front of Jack. He's not old enough to be hearin' them things," and with that she ran her hand over my head. Then she and my mother turned to walk back through the house the way they had come in. My mother looked back one last time, as if to say good-by to the walls, the history, the ghosts that still strode about the lopsided rooms, and then lowered herself off the porch, helping Nelle and me down after that. Crook stood looking questioningly at all three of us, then leapt off the three-foot high plateau and into a patch of goldenrod. He came out through the weeds and caught up to us as we made our way off the property and back onto the dirt road.

The visit to my mother's old home place over, all four of us ambled toward the main road which would take us back to the small farmhouse. When we reached the curve where we had seen the four doves take flight, we stopped.

"We should have come out earlier this morning," said Nelle. "Too hot at this time of day." My mother agreed and wiped her brow with a tissue she found in her pocket. It was at that moment that I felt something nudge my legs. My first thought was of the bad experience I had endured with the bull in the pasture, but I hadn't seen him around and I knew that my aunt and mother would have let out a yelp if they had noticed the beast was free and coming our way. Before I could react, Crook eased himself between my legs, crawling low to the ground. Then he rose up and lifted me a good three inches off the ground. Since he and I had done this routine before it was nothing new, but my mother and aunt had never seen it and they both doubled over again with laughter. Crook just looked at them and then up at me—he couldn't figure out what the problem was.

"Looks like you done got you a pony there, Jack," said Nelle when she had regained her composure. "Lord, the things that dog will let you do to him."

As if this weren't enough of a show for Crook to put on, he began to walk in the direction of the house and I had to try and balance myself. Since he wasn't a horse, I had no saddle, and as I was only ten, the mechanics of the thing took some time to master. By the time we arrived at the backdoor, I had pretty much figured out the process and I dismounted Crook like I had seen cowboys do in the western movies, swinging one leg up and over.

We didn't stay much longer that day, but returned several times over the next year. I guess my mother figured that I had experienced enough of the world she had grown up in, because after that first exploration of the ways of the farm, I wasn't asked to participate in any more chores. Jules and I played together often over the next series of visits, sometimes with Clement, sometimes not, but Jules was getting older and beginning to get interested in different things. He traded his cowboy outfits in for regular overalls again even though we still played in the backyard with Crook.

Five

One day about a year after my attempt at picking cotton and doing farm chores, we arrived for a visit. As usual, our car made its way down the dusty gravel road to my Aunt Vernelle's. We pulled up and, as was the custom, I opened my door and ran to the back of the house, up the steps and into the kitchen. No one was there.

I called out, but no one answered. Just as I was getting ready to give up, Nelle came from the back of the house and into the kitchen.

"How you a doin', Jack?" she asked, tousling my hair.

"Fine," I said, noticing that something was different, that something was wrong. I squinted my eyes, trying to see inside her demeanor, to see what was the matter. Then she spoke again.

"Why don't you run out back, out to the barn and get Jules," she said. "You can go play out in back of the pasture today. Bud's dynamited a new pond on Essie and Gilchrist's old place and y'all can go fishing."

"All right," I said, and swung open the screen door. I stood there on the porch for a minute, just looking around, and then I noticed that something was missing. "Crook!" I yelled, throwing my voice into the backyard and across the pasture. "Crook! Come 'ere boy, come on!" I waited but there was nothing. Just then my mother came up the back steps, carrying a grocery bag of store-bought items for Nelle.

"Jack, you don't need to be playing with that dog today. Go find Jules and have him teach you how to catch some of those catfish in that new pond they've built."

"But I want to play with Crook," I said. "Where is he?" My mother didn't say anything, but just went into the house. Now there was nothing separating me from the kitchen but the rusted screen door. Maybe they thought I had already run on to find Jules. Maybe they thought I wasn't paying attention. But for whatever reason, I overheard them.

"You didn't tell him?" I heard Nelle ask.

"I was hoping he would just forget about it," answered my mother. Then one of them must have seen me standing there, for the conversation stopped and something inside told me that I had to find out what was going on. I don't remember what happened next exactly, but I was tearing out across the pasture, completely oblivious to the cows and the bull that had so effortlessly nudged me out a year ago when Jules, Clement, and I had gone cow tipping.

I do remember reaching the barbed wire fence and maneuvering myself in between two ominous strands of gnarled metal, and then sailing through the small meadow smelling of wildflowers and grasses. The sun was intense and it drew from the foliage of the area a strange perfume—as if the earth itself had reached up through the living things and sunk hooks into your very soul by means of scent and sight.

I found the barn door handle and swung open the creaking door. Chickens squawked in their berths and the solitary horse kicked at the flimsy wooden side of the barn. The structure wasn't that sturdy, as it had always leaned slightly, and I didn't want to cause any disturbance that might result in the building's ruin, but I had to find Jules.

"Jules!" I called out, directing my voice upwards toward the loft. It was only a second until his head appeared above the hay. The sunlight caught the matching colors of his hair and that of the soft straw, and for a moment the two were almost indistinguishable.

"Hold on a minute," he said, and swung himself onto a rickety wooden ladder. Its bottom rung was almost directly at my feet and I waited for him to descend, noticing the backside of his ill-fitting overalls. He skipped the last three rungs and landed with a "plop" in front of me.

"Jules," I said, before he had a chance to speak, "where's Crook?" He didn't say anything, but just looked at me completely blank for a minute, as though he was totally caught off-guard by the question.

"Didn't nobody tell you?" he asked, with a look in his eye that said he hoped I had been given this information and the onerous chore would not be left up to him.

"Tell me what?" I asked, real fear rising in my voice. At this point I began to look around the barn, as though I expected to see the dog miraculously appear from behind a cow or bushel of corn husks.

"Come on," Jules said, and pulled me out the other end of the barn, toward where the new pond was. I acquiesced, walking in silence for a while, not sure whether or not to disturb the solitude, afraid what might come from it. After a while, unable to contain myself, I spoke.

"So?" I asked. "Where is he?" We were both standing at the edge of the pond. Jules bent down, picked up a small rock, and skipped it across the body of water. It sank and rose over the surface like a gull skimming for fish. Finally, about a third of the way from the pond's farthest edge, the stone gave up its flight and dove, one last time, into the dark and muddy water. Then Jules squinted up at the sun, and without looking at me, but while picking up another rock, said, "Old Crook's dead. Daddy had to shoot him. His back was broke," and with that he skipped another of his stones across the surface of the water. This one went even further, as if propelled by some anger or unfairness of life—it almost made it to the other side this time.

"What do you mean, 'His back was broke?' Who broke it?" I asked, completely oblivious to how such a thing might have come about. Jules didn't say anything, but he did skip another stone across the pond's surface. Of the three, it performed the worst, and with that Jules turned from the water's edge and I followed him back toward the pasture.

Neither of us said anything. We just walked dejectedly toward the house in silence with Jules occasionally swatting at some long waving tuft of grass or a dragonfly that happened to be too close. It was as if we were encased in some alien and tempered atmosphere which didn't allow us to discuss the dog and how his death had come about—Jules because of his anger and grief, and me because of guilt and fear.

Not much else happened that afternoon. We didn't stay long, and soon mother and I were making our way to the car. The quietness was too thick for all of us. She started the engine and the coldness from the air conditioner blasted my senses. I turned the vents directly on myself, hoping the freezing air would quell my emotions. But as soon as my mother turned the car around in the driveway and I saw Jules and my Aunt Nelle wave; as soon as I saw my Uncle Bud come out—hands in his back pockets—the tears began and I realized for the first time that Crook was dead and that at least some of his death was my doing. I turned my head toward the window to look at the fields which were browning in the hot Alabama sun; turned my head so that my mother would not see my tears. And I was now noticing the speed at which we were traveling as my mother swung the car onto the main highway, the very one that ran into the town of Moulton, which in turn ran into the street that the nursing home was on. As we drove by it, I felt a pang for anyone that had to end up there, never realizing that one day I would be paying it a visit, not as a patient, but as a relative of someone who was such a part of my life.

Six

"Mrs. Dadefyfe, it's time for me to change you after you've finished eating." It was one of the young women who worked in the nursing home that my Aunt Vernelle was in, and she brought me mentally back from the fields of Lawrence County to the stark, sterile concrete building that now housed one of the last living links to my past. Throughout my recollections and memory recall that had taken me back to her home and her life, I had managed to get Aunt Nelle to at least sample the Jell-O, and she had done quite well with the creamed corn and pieces of roast beef that I had cut up for her.

"Is that all you want now, Nelle?" I asked in an overly soft voice that people use for small children and animals. I knew that I wouldn't receive an answer. Then I turned to the woman who was still hovering in the doorway. "Just give me a few more minutes with her," I said, still holding the spoon at my aunt's mouth, " I want to see if I can get her to finish the creamed corn."

"Nelle, do you want any more of this? Do you want any more? Come on, Nelle, just one more bite. How about some of this grape juice?"

That seemed to do it. While the creamed corn and roast beef weren't a big hit today, the grape juice was. She held the plastic cup with both hands, the way a squirrel holds a nut, and slurped down the sugary liquid, the whole time her eyes turned up over the cup, looking into mine. When I tried to pry the cup from her hands, she started to cry.

"Don't cry, Nelle," I said. "I won't take it away. I won't take it away." Then I began to speak to her in a normal voice, not really knowing whether she could hear me or not, whether she could make sense of my words. As I spoke of nothing in particular—the weather, the new subdivision I had seen on the edge of town—I was going over in my mind exactly where I had been that day, before my visit to the nursing home.

I had driven by the house where Nelle and her family had lived and had even pulled my car into the drive the way my mother used to, hoping that if I performed the task just so, that the house, the barn, the pasture, all of it would appear again—at least for a moment—exactly as it once had been. Not having had the scene reconstruct itself to my liking, I had gotten out of the car and walked around the deserted property, finding the house smaller, the grass dryer, the pasture empty. About the only thing left was the sun which drew out the scent of milkweed and wildflowers.

I walked around to the back of the house. Only a breeze inhabited the area, and as I turned my attention to the now-remembered opening below the porch, I was reminded of that day Crook had shown me his hiding place and the artifacts he had stolen. I half-expected to find a blue rubber ball with teeth marks, or a half-eaten catcher's mitt, but there was only an empty space with the decaying remnants of pine needles that a German shorthaired pointer had collected in order to make himself a bed.

I had taken my leave after that discovery, and driven the eight miles into town to the nursing home. And now here I was, communing over a simple cup of grape juice with my mother's only sister.

"Nelle?" I asked, "do you remember the farm? Do you remember the time you took me to pick cotton?" There was nothing. No recognition at all. I wasn't disappointed. I knew it could be this way. Some days were good and some weren't. Occasionally you'd hit upon something, some one thing that might seem totally insignificant to you but that would set a light off in her eyes. When that happened, she was, for one brief instant, the old Vernelle, complete with all of her life experiences and memories. But then in the same instant, it was gone—sunk deep once again into the impenetrable depths of what was left of her mind.

I tried again. "Nelle? I'm thinking of buying a house in Courtland. Courtland's near Moulton. Do you remember Courtland? Do you remember Moulton? Nelle? Do you remember the time I came to stay with you? Mother and I came to stay with you? Do you remember, Nelle?"

Then I tried reaching back, pulling what I thought to be the one magic trick of memory that might do it. Something we had both associated with, some spirit borrowed from another dimension that had been a part of both our lives at certain points.

I took a deep breath and let it out. "Nelle? Do you remember old Crook? Do you remember that old dog that . . ." But before I could go on, before I could finish my attempt, something happened. I had said some enchanted word, some phrase of remembering, conjuring for her and me a one-time correlation of feelings, and now, for this one brief moment, her eyes were level with mine and we connected. That was the light, and for one transitory instant her eyes spoke to me. I could see she not only understood, but remembered, as if every detail from one of those hot summer days was fresh in her mind again—alive with the smell of the earth and animals, with baking, and the churning of butter, with caring for her family. Every blade of grass, every boll of cotton, the squirrel parts in the sink, the feel of the butter churn in her hands as the milk from the cows began to transform and change into something new—it was all there for that one brief moment, brilliant and intriguing, yet incomplete—

like the finding of a bird wing or broken arrowhead, each of which has its own story to tell if only the pieces could be put back together.

"Crook," I said again. "You remember Crook. Crook, that old dog you used to have, you remember him?" She was nodding now, remembering not only the dog, but other things which made their way to the surface, coming up as if having been raised up out of the water after a country baptism by some strong preacher's hand. She looked deep into my eyes and nodded. Then she was struggling with something. Her mouth twitched. Some air escaped. I stared into her eyes, not wanting to lose the moment, trying to ignore the surroundings: the construction paper giraffes with clothespin legs; the food cart rolling noisily about in the hallway; the sobbing of relatives who had just lost someone dear to them, standing just a little too close to the open door of Nelle's room; the withered and aging woman who stood in one place in the hall with a death grip on her walker, lolling her head from side to side over and over.

I too nodded, hoping Nelle would take some strength from me, anything that might give her what she needed to carry through with what it was she was trying to do. Then her lips came together and silently she formed a word. I bent my ear close to her so that she didn't have to strain.

"Tell me again?" I pleaded. "Tell it to me, Nelle." And the thing was borne aloft as softly as the flight of a passing dragonfly's wings near your ear on a warm summer day. The word came from her mouth and hung for that brief second in the air, suspended only by the hope of attainment of memories years back by her and me. By the miracle of God it passed through the space between her lips to my ears, and I took it in with the same relish a child has for his first Christmas or Easter—the long wait over, the receiving which now (only rarely) equals the anticipation.

Her lips struggled again. There was a pause that seemed to last for hours, but in reality was only a minute. Then it was born again, fresh and alive, like a timid but rejuvenated churchgoer at a tent revival.

"Crook," she said, as her mouth released the word, and she jerked her head slightly in a nod, as if to confirm that I had gotten what I had come for. She nodded again, and our eyes connected and reached back across the years of existence and pain and joy and suffering, until it brought us through that time together, right back to this moment.

I had been blessed with one word—a word that encompassed so much for the both of us. For me it was the memory of a dog that I had once known as a child, but in reality it was much more than that for it brought back to me an era when life was at its prime for my mother's sister and her family. They hadn't known it at the time, so busy were they living, but years later, as most of us are apt to do, they had looked back on that age and wondered where it had all gone. It was for me a time long ago when pieces of the South and my youth were quickly disappearing. It was a remembrance of something that had engraved itself so strongly on my being that I now felt that incredible mixture of guilt and disgrace and elation and expectation, all rolled into one big thing, that somehow fit into the universe and my life.

For Nelle it was all that and something more, for it was as if some thief in the night had stolen upon her while she slept, removing pieces of her life, only to give one of them back for this brief instant, in this one brief life, in this one brief nursing home in Moulton, Alabama. It was as if for one moment when her eyes lit up, we were both seeing a dog—a German shorthaired pointer, bounding tirelessly across an open field, free and young, full of the life that lay ahead for him, and her, and me.

About The Author: Jackson Tippett McCrae is originally from the South. After working for *Smithsonian Magazine*, Condé Nast Publications, and Miller Sports Group in New York, he moved to Connecticut where he currently resides. His first novel, THE BARK OF THE DOGWOOD, was published in May 2002 and is now in its second printing. He has also completed his second novel, another collection of short stories, and a screenplay.

Also by Jackson Tippett McCrae

The Bark of the Dogwood

A Tour of Southern Homes and Gardens

"Downright hysterical. An entertainment potpourri.
I couldn't stop reading."
The Sanford Herald

"Rich in complexity . . . not for the faint-hearted."
Southern Scribe

"Can make you laugh out loud . . . scenes with the
power to disturb and to haunt."
Echo Magazine

"Haunting, forceful, gripping, and intricate. This
kaleidoscopic and original book has everything going
for it—murder, blackmail, humor, love, grief, longing,
and insight into the human condition—a deftly created
triumph."
Peter Marino

"Thoroughly engaging novel . . . a highly recommended
and compelling tale."
Midwest Book Review

"This reader's interest was piqued, then held throughout
the book . . ."
Pine Bluff Commercial